How to Fool a Duke

The Husband Dilemma
Book 1

Mary Lancaster & Violetta Rand

DRAGONBLADE
PUBLISHING, INC.

Dragonblade Publishing, Inc. is an imprint of Kathryn Le Veque
Novels, Inc.
P.O. Box 7968
La Verne CA 91750
ceo@dragonbladepublishing.com

Produced in the United States of America

First Edition November 2020
Mass Market Paperback Edition

Dearest Reader;

Thank you for your support of a small press. At Dragonblade Publishing, we strive to bring you the highest quality Historical Romance from the some of the best authors in the business. Without your support, there is no 'us', so we sincerely hope you adore these stories and find some new favorite authors along the way.

Happy Reading!

CEO, Dragonblade Publishing

Additional Dragonblade books by Author Mary Lancaster

The Husband Dilemma Series
How to Fool a Duke

Season of Scandal Series
Pursued by the Rake
Abandoned to the Prodigal
Married to the Rogue
Unmasked by her Lover

Imperial Season Series
Vienna Waltz
Vienna Woods
Vienna Dawn

Blackhaven Brides Series
The Wicked Baron
The Wicked Lady
The Wicked Rebel
The Wicked Husband
The Wicked Marquis
The Wicked Governess
The Wicked Spy
The Wicked Gypsy
The Wicked Wife
Wicked Christmas (A Novella)

The Wicked Waif
The Wicked Heir
The Wicked Captain
The Wicked Sister

Unmarriageable Series
The Deserted Heart
The Sinister Heart
The Vulgar Heart
The Broken Heart
The Weary Heart
The Secret Heart
Christmas Heart

The Lyon's Den Connected World
Fed to the Lyon

Also from Mary Lancaster
Madeleine

CHAPTER ONE

S ARAH REACHED FOR the final note. She sang it with all the clarity she had been taught and all the emotion of which she was capable. And she held it perfectly before letting it fade into silence.

Exhilarated, she glanced toward Signor Arcadi. To her delight, he did not merely nod his grudging approval. He beamed. And then the applause broke out. Her audience rose en masse in spontaneous acclaim, rather than merely polite appreciation.

At last, she thought with anticipation. *At last, I am ready...*

She curtseyed deeply in gratitude, first to her audience and then to Signor Arcadi, who had trained her voice beyond a mere ladylike accomplishment to this level of skill and power. To have reached the stage of capturing this audience of cultured and talented people almost overwhelmed her.

"Better. Much better," Signor Arcadi murmured and placed her hand on his arm with gratifying pride. Together, they stepped forward to meet the adulation.

Sarah could almost imagine she had just sung at Covent Garden, instead of a tea-time recital in a small assembly room in the backwater town of Whitmore. Yet in many ways, these people congratulating her were her peers, and their opinion mattered nearly as much as Signor Arcadi's.

She was smiling so much; she thought her face would split. Hammy, more properly Miss Hammond, once her governess and now her companion, held her hands clasped under her chin in almost motherly pride.

The crowd parted, and she saw that her performance had been honored indeed. Lady Whitmore stood before her—a tiny lady, white haired and yet not quite elderly, supremely elegant in her simple silk gown and diamonds. As Sarah curtsied, Lady Whitmore extended her hand. Another accolade.

"You have always had one of the most beautiful voices I have ever heard," Lady Whitmore said kindly. "And now you are a credit to Signor Arcadi. A moving and utterly charming performance, my dear."

"Thank you, ma'am," Sarah said gratefully, taking her hand. "You are all kindness."

"And I am all pride," Signor Arcadi beamed. "My favorite pupil. Until tomorrow, at least, when we will go over your mistakes."

Sarah laughed. "Couldn't you leave it until then to take the wind out of my sails?"

"He is a hard taskmaster," Lady Whitmore agreed. "Which is why we so appreciate him here! Now my dear, I have an invitation for you. Would you care to dine with me this evening? Bringing Miss Hammy, of course."

"Thank you," Sarah said, dazed by this fresh honor. "I would love to."

"I'm afraid it will not be a dinner party, merely a cozy supper with just the three of us."

"I look forward to it," Sarah murmured. And she did. If only to tell Lady Whitmore that it was time for her to leave this sanctuary of art and culture, for it was time to take all her talents to the real world.

LADY WHITMORE WAS the undoubted queen of her domain. Her castle sat on top of the cliff overlooking the sea on one side and the town of Whitmore on the other. On a fine spring evening, it was a pleasant walk up the hill from Sarah's cottage. As she and Hammy drew closer, the castle seemed to lose its fairy-tale quality and become, instead, the defensive stronghold it was designed to be.

"It is as if she defends us all from up here," Sarah mused as they walked under the arch of the outer, thirteenth-century walls. "Only instead of violent raiders, she repels prying eyes and unwanted family."

"Yes, well, you must not speculate," Hammy warned her. "It was always part of the agreement when we took the cottage."

"We promised not to speculate about our neighbors," Sarah argued, "not about her ladyship."

"She is a neighbor, too," Hammy said firmly.

"Yes, but don't you wonder about her just a little? One would think she must be lonely up here by herself, and that is why she has made her village a sanctuary of the arts and learning for those others who care to hide from the world for whatever reasons. But she only moves among us occasionally, and even more rarely invites anyone to dine."

"You do not know how many people dine here," Hammy pointed out. "Or how often."

"Well, we have been here more than a year," Sarah pointed out, "and this is our first invitation. Do you suppose she knows we are leaving?"

The conversation had taken them across the wide courtyard which had been covered in lawns and gardens, to the front door, where Hammy frowned her to silence. There had been a time when Sarah would have sung at the top of her voice just for the fun of defying her, and she was still tempted. But she had learned good manners among everything else, so she merely smiled wryly and inclined her head while her old governess raised the large, iron knocker.

Almost at once, the great door swung open. A liveried, middle-aged footman bowed them inside, and Sarah looked about her in wonder. The entrance hall was a seamless blend of ancient carved stone and modern luxury. An indecipherable coat of arms carved above doorways, carpets on the stone floors, and even leading up the massive, curving staircase. Wall sconces looked as if they were made for flaming torches but contained candles.

An elderly, dignified butler materialized before them and asked them with a bow to follow him. He led them up the staircase and along a picture-lined gallery to a set of double-doors, which he pushed open.

He bowed into the room. "Your Grace. Miss Sarah and Miss Hammy."

Your Grace. Sarah's curiosity burgeoned. Their hostess, the sole occupant of the room before they walked in, was Lady Whitmore. Why would her servant address her as *Your Grace*? A title once reserved for queens, and now only for duchesses—among the female sex at least.

"Ah, thank you, Saunders," Lady Whitmore said. Smiling, she stood up from a massive desk at which she had been writing, and replaced her pen in the elegant stand. "Ladies, please join me in a glass of sherry. Or would you prefer ratafia?"

Sarah, dragging her gaze from the massive leather-bound books and what looked like parchment scrolls that lined the cabinets around the walls, curtseyed and asked for sherry.

Lady Whitmore served them herself from a Venetian glass decanter into matching glasses. "This is the center of my world," she said, presenting the glasses, and waving her hand around the room. "My library."

Sarah sat on the comfortable, velvet-covered sofa. "It is a beautiful room. Are you engaged upon a great work here?"

"Many minor works," Lady Whitmore replied.

"You have a wonderful view," Hammy said, gazing in awe toward the window that overlooked the sea.

"My inspiration and my reminder of a mere human's limitations," Lady Whitmore said, choosing a chair close to them.

"What are the subjects of your works?" asked Sarah, who had once believed women had no need of learning and that bluestockings were to be pitied.

"Genealogy," Lady Whitmore replied unexpectedly. "Largely. Also, I study human nature, which I suppose makes me a philosopher. We shall talk more of that over dinner, if you wish. But I would like to hear about you, Miss Sarah. Your little recital this afternoon was...dazzling."

"Thank you," Sarah said, blushing with gratitude. "I have worked hard over the last year."

"So Signor Arcadi tells me. Of course, he is delighted to have such a naturally sweet voice to train. But I understand you have not limited yourself to his training. You also attend lectures in art and the classic texts, poetry readings, and even the political salons. Your interests are wide."

"They are," Sarah agreed.

"And you, Miss Hammy? I believe you were Miss Sarah's governess? Are you responsible for her voracious love of learning?"

"I would like to claim so," Hammy said ruefully, "but in truth, it occurred in spite of me rather than because of me. I taught only the basic education and accomplishments thought to be necessary in a young lady of quality. And from the age of eleven, I'm afraid Sarah despised those things."

"I was, alas, selfish and opinionated," Sarah admitted. "And wild to a fault. I led poor Hammy in a terrible dance for the next five years."

"Oh, it was not as bad as that," Hammy insisted. "Although it must be said, you did worry your dear parents."

Lady Whitmore's perceptive gaze flickered from one to the other, although she kept her interested smile throughout. "Then what on earth led you to Whitmore? A positive hotbed of learning and accomplishments?"

"I grew up," Sarah said lightly and sipped her sherry.

"At the ripe old age of, what?" Lady Whitmore wondered. "Are you even nineteen years old yet?"

"Almost," Sarah admitted.

"Then you were just seventeen when you came to us, were you not? An age when most young ladies of your class are enjoying their first London Season and trying to catch a husband."

Sarah couldn't quite prevent the curl of her lip or the echo of the old hurt. "My parents did not feel I would compete well on the marriage mart. They sent me abroad with my aunt and uncle in the hope the experience would give me a little...polish."

"Did it?" Lady Whitmore asked innocently.

Sarah laughed. "In all honesty, no. But it did open my eyes to many things, mainly my own ignorance. I realized there was more to the world than climbing trees and doing exactly what I wished. I learned what I liked to do and what I was good at—singing. And I realized I needed to broaden my mind as well as my accomplishments. Somewhere along the way, I heard of

Whitmore, and when we came home, I asked Hammy to investigate for me. I am here with my parents' permission, although I suspect they tell their friends I am still abroad."

"Interesting," Lady Whitmore murmured.

Saunders, the dignified butler, opened the doors once more. "Dinner is served, Your Grace."

Again, Sarah had to swallow back her curiosity as they rose and accompanied Lady Whitmore to a dining room that was not the huge banqueting hall Sarah expected, but a pleasant, comfortable room with another charming view of the sea under the darkening sky.

"I prefer to dine here with my guests," Lady Whitmore said. "Since comfort is so much more important than formality."

The servants withdrew after serving each course, which added further to the sense of intimacy. At first, Lady Whitmore's conversation was impersonal and pleasantly humorous. Only when the fish course had been cleared away and a game pie set before them, did their hostess ask Sarah, "So, have you found what you wanted to at Whitmore?"

"Yes, I believe I have. And I fear we shall be leaving quite soon."

"We shall miss you. Might I ask what you intend to do?"

"Go back to the real world," Sarah said wryly, "and implement my new…knowledge."

Lady Whitmore raised one intrigued eyebrow. "In what way?"

"In the way I always meant to."

Lady Whitmore, who ate sparingly, laid down her knife and fork. "I would be honored to know what that is. As you may have guessed, I like to help my guests when I can, even when they leave us. Of course, you are under no obligation to reveal anything, but I have watched you grow and blossom here, and I hope I may be of some use to you. I know who you are, of course, but not the true motivation behind your long stay with us."

Sarah shifted uncomfortably and reached for her wine. Without lifting the glass, she said, "I believe I am afraid to lose your good opinion. You will think me petty, and perhaps you are right, but I came to prove something to myself and to my family. And to…a certain high-ranking gentleman."

"Perhaps you should begin at the beginning," Lady Whitmore said calmly. "Which is that you were born Lady Sarah Merrington, the youngest daughter of the Earl of Drimmen."

Sarah inclined her head with mock pride. "I shall not bore you with the story of my life! It will bring back too many horrible memories for poor Hammy here. I was something of a wild child. My brothers and sisters were much older, and so I played with local children at Merrin Park—the family estate where I was largely brought up. Most of my friends were village boys and farmers' sons. One day, when I was about sixteen, my parents noticed me and were appalled. They decided I should learn to be a lady, and poor Hammy tried again to drum some manners and etiquette into me."

"She could behave very well when she chose," Hammy put in.

Sarah cast her a quick, apologetic smile. "Well, it made Hammy unhappy when I behaved badly, so I tried not to. Then, before I was even out, my parents arranged a possible—and brilliant—match for me. With the high-ranking gentleman I mentioned before." She sipped the wine thoughtfully and set down the glass. "I should probably say that I had seen my older sisters make advantageous matches that made them neither happy nor interesting people, so I resolved that if I was to marry the duke, he would have to like me as I am."

"Which is to say a wild, self-willed but caring child?" Lady Whitmore suggested.

Sarah blinked in surprise at the last epithet, though Hammy said warmly, "Exactly."

Sarah shrugged. "So, the day he came to Merrin Park, I hid up a tree and watched for his arrival. I threw crab apples at his carriage as it drove through the grounds. The coachman was furious with me and stopped especially to tell me off."

"Did you throw an apple at him, too?" Lady Whitmore inquired.

"No, I was running short of apples and was saving them for the duke, who eventually stepped down himself. Surprisingly, he seemed more amused than anything else." Sarah paused, remembering her first sight of Leonard Blackmore, the young Duke of Vexen. The world had tilted with only half-understood excitement, for he was not staid and self-important at all. He was tall and handsome with laughing eyes and a mouth very ready to smile.

"*Did* you throw the apple at him?" Lady Whitmore asked.

Sarah smiled. "I did. Knocked his hat off, too. But he just picked it up, and the next two apples I threw, he caught in the hat. Then he sent the carriage on and climbed up the tree. For a moment, I thought he'd come to punish the impudent village girl, but he didn't. I told him who I was, and he laughed and sat on the branch beside me."

"He sounds...fun," Lady Whitmore said as Sarah stopped talking to eat.

"He was," Sarah replied, when she had swallowed. "In fact, we got on so well that I resolved to be on my best behavior for the rest of his visit. I dressed in my finest gown for dinner, even let the maid curl my hair, and then went to my parents and told them I would do it. I would marry the duke."

She paused again, trying not to feel the hurt and humiliation she had known two years ago. The hard, little shell of anger and vengeance saved her once more. "He had already left Merrin Park. He told my father he could not consider marriage with me because I was a hoyden, that he needed a well-bred and cultured wife fit for the best drawing rooms in Europe."

Lady Whitmore blinked. "That seems a shocking turnaround from the man who climbed a tree to laugh and joke with you."

Sarah shrugged carelessly. "Apparently, I was amusing enough for outdoor entertainment but not fit for his drawing room."

Lady Whitmore sat back in her chair, while the servants came in and cleared the game pie away. They brought in desserts and again departed.

"And so, you decided to become what he wanted?" Lady Whitmore guessed. "What your family wanted. A young lady of culture and accomplishment who outshines all others?"

"More or less."

"Just so that he will marry you?" Lady Whitmore said with a hint of pity.

Sarah laughed. "Oh, dear me, no. So that he will beg me on bended knee to marry him. And fully appreciate the humiliation of rejection."

CHAPTER TWO

"YOU HAVE GONE to a lot of trouble," Lady Whitmore observed when she had recovered her breath, "for what you rightly call a petty revenge."

"It is not just for him," Sarah admitted. "It's also for my parents. I want them to see if they like me as they wanted me to be."

"You think you have grown...above them?" Lady Whitmore asked.

Sarah considered. "No, not above. I am still Sarah underneath all the manners and the learning and accomplishments. But I might not want them to see that immediately."

Again, she had the impression that her hostess's steady eyes saw straight through to her soul.

"You are right," Sarah said abruptly. "It is petty and vengeful."

"And will do the hurt child a lot of good while exerting no lasting damage on the parents who neglected her and then rejected who she had grown into?"

Sarah's breath caught. "You are…incisive."

A smile flickered on Lady Whitmore's lips. "And the young man? The duke? His punishment is a broken heart. Is that not lasting damage?"

"I considered that," Sarah said. "But, no, I don't think so. A man as shallow as he turned out to be has no feelings deep enough to be hurt so very badly. It will hurt his pride and perhaps make him miserable for a week or so."

"And that is enough for you?"

"It is, now. To be honest, somewhere in this last year, my motives changed. I still want my revenge, but the journey I took is for *me*. And in the real world, I believe I can find happiness from that."

Lady Whitmore looked thoughtful, which was at least better than disgusted. "So, you would seek him out at *ton* parties and captivate him? In public? While becoming the rage of London?"

"That is my plan."

"Hmm." Lady Whitmore spooned syllabub into her mouth. "Delicious. One thing more, Lady Sarah. Dukes—particularly young dukes—are not so thick on the ground. Would I be correct in assuming yours is the Duke of Vexen?"

Sarah hesitated, but she already told everything else. She nodded, and Lady Whitmore's gaze fell to the table.

"I would like to make a suggestion," she said at last. "In the past, I have helped other young ladies in various difficult situations by inviting certain gentlemen to events here in Whitmore. It is a much more discreet form of matchmaking than the hectic marriage market in London. So no one here will think it odd if I invite his grace to the exhibition of paintings we hold next month. In fact, we might ask him to open it formally. And then you may conduct your revenge in the safety of this sanctuary, without any loss of reputation."

"Here?" Sarah frowned. "I never thought of that."

"It means you may leave Whitmore with a clean slate, if you like. And carry on with your life unencumbered by the ill-feelings of the past."

Sarah mulled that over, then glanced at Hammy, who nodded once. Lady Whitmore's scheme did have advantages. The grand, public humiliation she had once planned for the duke, no longer seemed so important. But nor could she let the slight go unanswered. He would have to learn.

"Very well," she said. "Thank you. I will take up your offer. Providing the duke answers your invitation, of course."

"Of course. I shall set it in motion."

It was odd, for although Lady Whitmore spoke with her usual calm friendliness, when she raised her wine glass to her lips, her hand seemed to tremble.

"YOU DID NOTICE the slight tremor in Lady Whitmore's hand as she discussed the duke?" Sarah looked Hammy over, always waiting for her delayed reaction to things. Her former governess wore her heart on her sleeve, so her opinion could be counted as honest.

"I did," Hammy said rather tight-lipped. "Our gracious hostess appeared greatly troubled, if not saddened by your wish for revenge on His Grace."

"Perhaps she is acquainted with his family? Or maybe she has experienced something similar to my own past, and it hurt her to relive the memory?"

Her companion shook her head. "I sense something deeper than that in her."

"Oh?" Sarah stopped walking and stared at Hammy. "What would that be?"

"I do not wish to speak out of turn, so I will not explain any further, not until I am sure of myself."

Sarah frowned, impatient as she had always been. In fact, she stamped her foot but then quickly corrected her bad behavior. "I am sorry."

A demure smile brightened Hammy's face. "There is the young woman who has matured this last year."

Sarah sighed. "Yes, she is inside me, but so is the spoiled, impudent child I have always been."

Her companion squeezed her hand affectionately. "I am proud of you. I do not believe you would have admitted such a thing six months ago."

"Perhaps not. Yet, I find myself still wanting to be that spoiled girl."

"You cannot serve two masters, Sarah."

"Whatever do you mean by that?"

"Only that you must choose which person you wish to be more. The girl throwing apples, or the lady ready to face the world and win the admiration of her peers."

Sarah knew what resonated most in her heart. Becoming a graceful member of society. Yet... Temptation beckoned her nearly every minute of every day. If no one expected much from her, then she needn't expect much from herself. But the duke... She envisioned him, that warm smile, those pleasant eyes, and his broad shoulders—so handsome, so physically appealing.

What would it feel like to bring him to his knees? To experience him falling in love with her, to want her after that embarrassing rejection? She did not hate him, but neither did she appreciate his unfair judgement. Her tender feelings for him had been instantaneous after he climbed the tree and sat beside her. She bit her bottom lip and looked away from Hammy, an undeniable tear in the corner of her eye.

"Sarah?"

She tried to wave her away.

"Do you forget how well I know you?" Hammy asked quietly.

"Of course, not," she admitted. "That is why I looked away from you. I do not wish you to see me cry."

"Dearest." Hammy's comforting arms came around her, pulling her into a tight embrace. "If you could find it within yourself to let go these negative feelings for the duke, we could make arrangements to travel back to London at the end of the week. No one need know the true nature of our stay here."

The softest part of Sarah considered her suggestion sincerely. Forgiveness was a virtue she hadn't quite mastered yet. It was also something Lady Whitmore hadn't provided instruction on. Why should she give up the one thing that had inspired her to persevere during her time in Whitmore? The one purpose that had given her the courage to sing and study her art until she could not hold herself upright some evenings when she returned home to the cottage. No, Hammy was asking too much from her.

The Duke of Vexen needed to learn a valuable lesson, and Sarah would be the one to teach him, if not for herself, for the next young lady whose heart he might break.

CHAPTER THREE

T HE DUKE OF Vexen sat in his study, holding an elegant invitation in one hand, his brandy glass in the other. Usually he relished the idea of attending art exhibitions, but where in hell was this village called Whitmore? And how had Lady Whitmore become aware of his dedication to the arts and chosen to ask him to be the guest of honor at her event?

Of course, being a duke might have a hand in it, but Leonard was a discreet sort, private to a fault. His generous donations to various institutions around the country were given anonymously, and only his closest friends and family knew anything about how he spent his money.

Leonard had sponsored many an artist and opera singers—even a ballet dancer who became internationally famous four years ago after a stunning performance in Italy. But this? A private musicale and art exhibition at a castle in a seaside village he had never heard of? Should he even consider it? Would he discover another Mozart? Perhaps even another Michelangelo? That possibility titillated him more than sheer curiosity about the hostess.

"Well, Your Grace?" his secretary, Mr. James, asked politely. "How shall I respond to the lady?"

Leonard shrugged, dropped the invitation on his desk, and swallowed the last of his brandy. "Where is this place?"

"Some two hundred miles from London, Your Grace. It is located along the North Sea, I believe, where Vikings once lived." Mr. James lowered his spectacles down his nose and gave the duke a smile.

"Vikings?"

"I know how you feel about the possibility of looking into the archaeological activities in a place ripe with history."

Leonard snorted. "All of Britain should be an archaeological site, should it not, Mr. James?"

"Quite right, Your Grace. But Vikings are you favorite, I believe."

"Yes," he said, thinking about his private collection of artifacts from around the world, including Scandinavia. "Perhaps we should attend the event after all, Mr. James. Broadening my social circle to include Lady Whitmore might be beneficial. Please accept her invitation immediately."

Mr. James nodded and turned around on his chair at his desk that sat across the generous study from the duke's enormous mahogany desk. The space was more than a study really; it was an ante chamber to the magnificent library that possessed a collection of ancient manuscripts that might rival the Vatican's collection.

Leonard smiled to himself—it had taken ten generations to bring his family's collection of antiquities to where it stood today. Manuscripts, sculptures, paintings, fossils, and so much more. He prided himself on that—now if he could only find the perfect duchess to add to his flawless collection.

He stood abruptly and opened the carved, heavy doors that led into the library. The doors had been purchased from a crumbling, thirteenth century castle in Ireland and shipped to London and fitted inside his townhouse in Mayfair. His home encompassed three townhouses that had been made into one, providing the room and privacy he required to feel comfortable in such a boisterous and filthy city, though he loved it dearly.

He stopped in front of a shelf containing maps and chose an atlas covering Britain. He opened it on a table at the center of the room and searched the northeast coast for Whitmore, his eyes sweeping the map three times before he found it.

"Whitmore," he said aloud, then read what notes were included about the village. "Established in the ninth century as a trading post, eventually captured by the Norse in 966…"

He sighed. "Intriguing."

"What is intriguing, Your Grace?" Mr. James called from the doorway.

Leonard turned to gaze at his loyal secretary. "You were correct about Whitmore—there is a long history to the place. The more I think about it, the more I wish to see it. In fact, perhaps we should arrange to arrive early."

Mr. James cleared his throat. "How early?"

"Have Williams prepare my things. We leave at first light."

As soon as he awoke on his first morning at Whitmore Castle, Leonard knew he had made the right decision. Although difficult to discover, the castle was genuinely magnificent. And despite arriving late at night a full day before he was invited, he and James had been shown immediately to their rooms.

Poor James, who had never got used to the speed with which Leonard preferred to travel, had tottered immediately to bed, while Leonard, lamp in hand, had explored the environs, admiring the stone work and the tasteful nature of the restoration work. He had seen enough to inspire him, to wake with a glow of scholarly excitement.

Rising from his huge bed, he padded across the cold floor and threw wide the shutters. His bedchamber looked out onto the sea, and he could almost imagine a fleet of longboats sailing toward the shore. He expected some Viking warrior's wooden hall had once graced this hill, long before the Normans came with their passion for stone castles.

Leonard turned reluctantly away from the view. Discovering a silken rope, he tugged it, in the hope it would summon Clive, his valet. It did, although the man took some time to arrive, panting from his exertions.

"I'm to tell you Lady Whitmore will join you in the breakfast room, Your Grace," he said breathlessly. "I'll show you the way when you are ready."

Finally, washed, shaved and dressed with his usual smart propriety, Leonard followed his valet through the large outer room that appeared to be part of his suite, and beyond to a wooden staircase and a wide passage that led to an open door on the left. Their footsteps echoed. They met no one else on their journey.

And when Clive bowed him into the breakfast room, he discovered there only two elderly ladies, who appeared to be arguing.

They broke off at once, staring at him. He bowed, and they rose to their feet. One curtseyed. The other, a small, silver-haired lady with oddly piercing blue eyes, hurried toward him. At one point, she seemed to steady herself against the long, polished table, but otherwise gave no impression of frailty.

Her gaze clung to him, almost greedily. No doubt she was starved of company.

"Your Grace," she said, sinking in a regal curtesy before offering her hand. "I am Lady Whitmore. Forgive my failure to welcome you last night."

"There is nothing to forgive," he assured her. "And certainly not from a guest who arrives so inconveniently late at night."

"I trust you were made comfortable?"

"Extremely. Please, don't let me keep you from your breakfast."

"Breakfast is informal here," she told him pleasantly. "Please help yourself from the sideboard, and if there is anything else you might require, I will send for it. Oh, and this is my companion, Miss Frobe. May I pour you coffee? Or tea?"

Leonard bowed to the austere Miss Frobe, requested coffee, and began piling his plate from the many delicious-smelling dishes on offer.

"Your other guests—like my friend James— appear to be late risers," he observed, sitting opposite the ladies and lifting his knife and fork.

Lady Whitmore smiled. "I have no other guests."

Leonard paused. "I understood this was to be a major exhibition with many subscribers to the event."

"Oh, it is," Lady Whitmore replied. "But only you, as my guest of honor, are staying at the castle. There is a very comfortable inn, and the village is always full of talented artists and connoisseurs."

"I see." He inclined his head. "Then I feel doubly honored." *I think!*

Lady Whitmore sipped from a delicate porcelain cup. "It is only right when you are formally opening the event for us. The finishing touches are being put to the exhibition today. You may like to go and look at them before the opening tomorrow."

"What exactly is expected of me?" he asked bluntly.

"Just a few words of appreciation, and perhaps a toast?"

"I could probably manage that, though certainly an advance look at the exhibits will be in order," He just hoped they would not be so awful that he would struggle for something pleasant to say.

AFTER THE ALMOST heavy peace of the castle, the village appeared positively bustling when Leonard walked down with James later in the day. Among the few ordinary working folk was a surprisingly large number of ladies and gentlemen. Most of them were unknown to him, but some did look vaguely familiar. However, none appeared to recognize him, which was unusual for the Duke of Vexen. People passed with civil nods and polite murmurs of "Good afternoon," but he detected no curiosity or even much interest.

He decided he rather liked the anonymity.

James pointed to the far end of the village square. "That large building must be the assembly rooms her ladyship spoke of."

"I believe you are right. Is such an edifice not somewhat incongruous in such surroundings?"

"Unusual, certainly," James agreed.

A large bill on the front doors of the assembly rooms proclaimed the exhibition of art and musical evening tomorrow. The doors were locked, but opened promptly to James's knock.

"His Grace of Vexen, to see the exhibits," James said grandly, and the door was at once thrown wide.

Beyond a vestibule was a large gallery lined

with framed pictures and dotted with sculptures.

"We'll be building Your Grace a little plat-form just *there*," claimed the man who had admitted them and closed the door hastily behind them again, "where you can address the guests." He flung one hand to the door on the left. "That is the musical room. And there, at the end of the gallery, is the banqueting hall."

"Banqueting hall?" Leonard repeated, amused. "It sounds very grand."

The man grinned. "It isn't, but it's big enough, and there will be an excellent spread. We have some wonderful cooks. I'll leave Your Grace to look around. Shout if you need anything at all!"

Leonard, expecting very little, moved toward the first picture. What he really wished to do was return to the castle and explore further, and to potter in Lady Whitmore's considerable library to discover what he could about pre-Norman settlements here.

But the charming water color depicting the natural harbor and the sea caught his attention. So did the portrait of the old fisherman, and the sculpture of the child.

"I'll tell you what, James," he began with considerably more enthusiasm, "these..." He broke off as a pure, clear, feminine voice sounded from the closed door on the left. At first it was a single high note. Then the unknown woman sang a scale, up and down again. A man's muffled voice spoke, a pianoforte sounded, and the woman began to sing again.

Her exquisite voice sent chills of pleasure down his spine. Without a word, he strode past James and across the gallery to the door, determined to get closer.

A surprisingly young lady stood in the center of the room, hands folded casually in front of her as the most divine sounds he had ever heard slipped sweetly from her lips. Such a voice could make one weep with joy or sorrow. Already it caught at his breath. And that was before he really looked at her.

Night-black hair and creamy skin, a face of almost sculptured beauty, from her large, brilliant eyes to the soft, shapely lips from which fell such enchanting music. She was simply lovely.

And Leonard, for the first time in his life, was utterly dazzled.

She. She is the one.

>>>><<<<

SARAH'S VOICE STOPPED, quite without her permission. She could not breathe.

This was not how he was supposed to see her! She should be in her most elegant evening gown with her hair dressed *à la Grèque*. She should be singing with confidence, at her absolute finest. Not practicing scales and trying out snippets of songs to see where in the room her voice sounded best.

But at least he was gazing at her. As if he couldn't look away. Her heart missed a beat. Her chin came up in the haughty look she had practiced so long in front of the mirror.

And Arcadi, bless him, exploded to her rescue.

Throwing up his hands, he strode across the room, demanding, "Who in God's name are you to interrupt us?"

The duke's superior black eyebrow twitched upward, though he did not take his eyes off Sarah. "Vexen. In God's name or anyone else's, who are you?"

"Arcadi. And I command you to go!"

At last the duke's gaze released her. She didn't know whether she was relieved or disappointed to have lost his attention.

"Fernando Arcadi?" he said, frowning in apparent surprise. "Why yes, so you are. I heard you sing at Covent Garden."

"You are to be congratulated," Arcadi pronounced. "And if you don't get out this instant, you will never hear anyone sing again, least of all my pupil. Shoo!"

For the first time a hint of amusement entered the duke's intense dark eyes. "My good man, I am not a goose." He bowed to Sarah. "I beg you will forgive the interruption. Good day."

Sarah seemed to be rooted to the spot. What she wanted to do was throw him a careless nod of dismissal, but that would hardly have displayed her newly exquisite manners. She dropped a rather rigid curtsey and waited for the door to close behind him. Then, she tottered to the nearby stool and sank down on it before she fell. Her whole body was shaking.

This is ridiculous! How am I supposed to take revenge when a mere glimpse of him does this to me?

Of course, it was just the shock of seeing him. No one had told her he was in Whitmore yet... Well, the next time she would be ready.

Arcadi was so irritated with her distraction that he ended the rehearsal early and stormed off, stating that he washed his hands of her.

"No, you don't," she said affectionately. "And I promise I will be better tomorrow."

"Ha!" said Arcadi from the open door.

Sarah, her heart beating fast, took her time donning her pelisse, bonnet, and gloves, and replacing her music in its case. Then she walked out of the room and into the gallery.

She saw him at once near the front door. He could have been waiting for her—or he could just have been examining the pictures. Either way, he swerved to intercept her.

He bowed.

She inclined her head.

Since the porter was not present, he opened the front door for her.

She sailed past him, murmuring, "My thanks, sir. Good afternoon."

"How fortunate that we leave together," he observed. "I may now escort you to your destination."

She glanced at him, and found her way. "But it does not appear to be fortunate at all, sir. You forgot your hat."

"No, I didn't. I chose to abandon it in favor of your company,"

"Then it was a foolish choice, sir, for I do not need to be escorted the few steps to my lodging."

"I was not thinking of need but of pleasure."

She allowed a hint of amusement into her eyes. "What pleasure could a lady take in the escort of an improperly dressed gentleman?"

His lips quirked. "Perhaps it depends on the gentleman. Do you know, you seem strangely familiar? I believe we have met before."

"Really?" she said with polite boredom.

"My name is Vexen."

"How do you do?"

"And you?" he prompted.

She stopped at the garden gate of the cottage she shared with Hammy, and smiled. "My name? Since you claim to know me, sir, you must know that, too. I thank you for your escort. Good day."

As she turned away, she caught the gleam of appreciative laughter in his eyes, and knew with elation that she had at least caught his interest. But as she fumbled with the latch of the gate, he reached out and opened it for her. For an instant, his hand trapped hers, and it was she who could not breathe, for he stood too close.

He was taller than she remembered, more overwhelmingly physical. And when she cast a determinedly cool glance up at him, his smile was not boyish at all. If she had grown up, so had he.

He freed her hand and pushed open the gate.

"Thank you," she murmured and walked up the path in some confusion. *But I will win. I will bring you to your knees, even if only for a day.*

THERE WAS SOMETHING oddly familiar about the beautiful woman with the voice of an angel. Her eyes were the most compelling feature she possessed, a mix of sincerity and mischievousness, confidence and innocence. He watched her cross the threshold of the cottage, an older woman standing in the archway stared out at him. So, she was a proper lady—though it did not dissuade him from wanting to find out who she was, it did make it a bit inconvenient.

Undoubtedly, she would be singing at the

musicale tomorrow evening. And for his part, he'd be seated in the front row next to his gracious hostess, Lady Whitmore.

Smiling to himself, he set off for the castle with a renewed vigor to discover the mysteries of the ancient structure and its mistress.

To his surprise, Mr. James met him halfway home.

"Is everything all right, Mr. James?"

"Yes, sir. But the news I carry is too exciting to keep from you another moment."

The reason Mr. James and he got on so well was that the man had as much exuberance for history as he did, and it showed now in his disheveled appearance, sweat on his brow from rushing to find him.

"What news?"

"There is a burial ground—more precisely a mound, along the east side of the property, by the water."

"How did you find out this information, Mr. James?"

"Lady Whitmore invited me for tea, and we discussed your interest in the arts and history. She seemed rather pleased about it and opened up her library to me, to us, Your Grace."

"What else did you discover?"

"That the lady has given us her blessings to not only excavate the area as we see fit, but has offered to sell you whatever artifacts we recover at a flat rate."

"Flat rate?" He would never take advantage of a lady. She obviously didn't have any idea how much artifacts could be worth to the right collector or even the museums in London. "I do hope you thanked her for the generous offer but declined."

"Declined which part, sir?"

"The fee."

"Well…" Mr. James gazed at the ground and kicked at the dirt with the tip of his boot. "When I started to reject the offer…"

"She is a keen woman, is she not, Mr. James?"

"Incredibly so, Your Grace. Collected and calm, seems to rule this village with little effort, so much so, wherever I go, no one has an ill word for her. She seems to be the perfect mistress."

"Indeed." Leonard rubbed his chin. Everyone had a story to tell, secrets to hide. Especially those who appeared too perfect. "In any case, we will accept her offer to dig, but will settle a fair price once we find something of value, if we do at all."

Mr. James smiled. "A Viking burial mound, Your Grace. Imagine what we shall find there."

"I do not wish to disturb any bodies, for you know how I feel about that."

"Yes, sir. I am well aware that Lord Ainsworth's untimely death while investigating native burial grounds in America has left you a bit superstitious about curses." The secretary tried to supress a grin but failed miserably.

"You find it amusing?"

"I find it rather endearing, Your Grace."

"Endearing?" he uttered, revolted.

The secretary cleared his throat. "Allow me to correct my poor choice of word. Admirable."

Admirable was an acceptable alternative to endearing. By God, he still had a pair of bollocks—leave endearing qualities to old women and children.

Mr. James reached into his jacket and produced a crudely, hand-drawn map. "This will direct us to the area where the burial mound is located."

Leonard took the paper from him and looked it over, excitement firing his blood as it always did whenever opportunity presented itself. "Let us go, then, Mr. James."

"WHAT IS IT, Sarah?" Lady Whitmore called to her as she stared out the window, watching the gray waves crash over the boulders along the shoreline. That is how she felt at the moment, nervous and turmoil-stricken. The duke had turned her plan upside down. Just one wicked smile from the man had sent her running home like a frightened school girl.

Considering she usually had plenty to say, when she faced Lady Whitmore and couldn't find the right words...

"The duke is a striking man, is he not?"

She nodded.

"I take it your reunion was lively?"

"He is a rake."

Lady Whitmore arched a brow. "That is a rather serious accusation. You have not had a lot of exposure to the world of men, Sarah. Perhaps you mean arrogant or a notorious flirt but not a rake."

"He invaded the practice room at the assembly rooms and caused Arcadi to get into quite a bad mood."

Her hostess chuckled. "The wind could blow the wrong direction and that man would become agitated."

Sarah smiled. Her teacher was the epitome of any successful artist—overly sensitive, demanding, and brilliant. "Yes, I suppose you are correct on all counts. But the duke not only ended my practice once Arcadi stormed out and left me alone, as I went to leave, I discovered His Grace waiting for me without his hat!"

"There is nothing worse than finding an improperly dressed duke waiting for you!"

Had she heard her hostess properly? Or was her mind playing tricks on her. Surely such a refined woman as Lady Whitmore would never refer to a man in any state of undress, especially to an unmarried girl. "Did you…"

"Of course I did." Lady Whitmore invited her to sit next to her on the settee. "Even a woman of my years has an eye for handsome men. And the Duke of Vexen is every bit a charming and commanding specimen."

"Specimen?"

"Yes, like a science experiment."

That made Sarah relax, and she let out a sigh of relief. "I did not know how to respond to his inquiries. He swore we had met before."

"Well, you have!"

"I know."

"You are a hard girl to forget, Sarah."

"Am I?" The observation surprised her.

Lady Whitmore turned in her seat to get a better view of her. "You have reverted back to the unsure girl I met a year ago. Does this duke possess such power over you, my dear?"

Sarah gazed down at her unsteady hands folded on her lap. *Yes, he does.* "Perhaps." Her voice trembled.

"Listen to me." Lady Whitmore lifted her chin gently. "You are a beautiful girl, Sarah. Witty, talented, physically appealing, and very young. Men will naturally respond to your very presence in a room, much more so if you engage them in conversation. You must learn to control your emotions. Never let a man see you squirm—if you do, he will take advantage of you, even the best-intentioned gentleman."

"Even a duke?"

"Especially a duke."

CHAPTER FOUR

LEONARD EYED THE sea with deep admiration. To think Vikings had crossed that body of water centuries ago in open longships and landed in a strange, inhospitable country and taken it so easily. It intrigued him, almost made him wish he had been born at a different time.

"Your Grace." Mr. James's voice broke his concentration. "If you look up that embankment, I believe you can see an unnatural shape in the landscape. A slope that is too perfect."

Leonard followed his secretary's gaze and squatted down to get a clearer view. Yes, he believed the man was right. Waves, wind, and rain would have abraded the slope over the centuries. Something underneath the layers of soil provided protection for the mound. "I am in agreement with you, Mr. James. But is it worth investigating? We would need to hire local men to help excavate a large portion of the hill. That could lead to us spending more time than I had planned here."

"I have nowhere else to be, Your Grace."

Leonard gave him a lopsided smile, ever the jester whether intentional or not. "Then it is settled. The day after the exhibition, we will begin to assemble a team." He picked up a handful of silty soil and smelled it. Rich with nutrients and damp from the wet air. Sometimes Leonard thought he would have made a better gentleman farmer than a duke, for he appreciated every aspect of nature—every facet of the human spirit.

It was why he supported the arts, and why he took deep interest in history. Or maybe he and his ancestors were lacking any memorable talents and instead spent their wealth to surround themselves with people and objects that made them feel important and useful.

He shook that doubt aside. Leonard possessed natural talents—he had a sharp eye for beauty, an ear for music, and a voracious appetite for women. That took great stamina. And a few other unsavory skills. He smiled.

"What is it, Your Grace?"

"Just a private thought, Mr. James."

His secretary nodded. "Is it the nameless beauty you encountered at the assembly rooms?"

Why had he given his secretary the right to speak freely with him? No one would dare challenge a duke as he did. But it was yet another of many qualities he admired about his secretary. "Yes, Mr. James, she is on my mind."

"I could see that without getting confirmation from you, sir."

"Indeed."

Leonard stood and waved toward the castle. In need of a bath and perhaps a short rest before the formal dinner tonight, he started to walk back, followed closely by Mr. James.

"Why not ask our hostess about the girl?"

"It would be most improper, I think."

"Why, sir?"

"What if she is related to Lady Whitmore? I do not wish her to think I am ogling the young lady."

"But you were."

Mr. James stopped in his tracks and shook his head.

"What now?"

"You are a confusing man at times, sir."

"And you live vicariously through me, your employer."

The two men laughed and continued the trek back to the castle.

FROM THE WINDOW seat, Sarah glimpsed two

men stride across the courtyard, deep in conversation. At first, she thought they were her ladyship's servants, for the taller was in his shirt sleeves, his coat slung carelessly over one shoulder. But something in the impetuous grace of his stride caught her attention, reminding her suddenly of the young man who had leapt out of his coach as she threw apples at it.

Her heart lurched. She actually pressed her forehead to the glass in an attempt to see better. Laughing, he clapped his companion on the back, and they both disappeared from her view.

"It is," she blurted. "It is *him*! My lady, is the duke staying here in the castle?"

"Why, where else would he stay?" Lady Whitmore asked, amused.

"But...you mean he will join us for dinner?"

Lady Whitmore lifted one eyebrow. "It would be odd if he did not. You appear distraught."

Sarah pulled herself together with an embarrassed little laugh. "Of course not. I welcome the challenge."

"Do you?"

"Of course! It's just... making plans while hundreds of miles away from him is not quite the same as being face to face with him."

Lady Whitmore smiled faintly. "Certainly, he is an imposing young man, a man of distinction and power whom it would be foolish to take lightly." She hesitated, then beckoned to her. "My dear, there are many ways in which gentlemen can take advantage of a woman. The law regards us as inferior to men, but we are not powerless, and we should never throw away such power as we do have. So, you have to decide. Do you want power over him? Do you want him at your feet? Do you want to be friends? Will you just walk away from your revenge? You still have total freedom to choose."

"Of course, I will not walk away," Sarah said at once. She straightened her back. "He took me by surprise, but I shall be ready for him now." *I am an educated lady of culture, accomplishments, and refinement,* she told herself severely. *I am easily a match for him.*

The door opened then, but only to admit Hammy and Miss Frobe, Lady Whitmore's companion, who had been discussing potted plants in the latter's sitting room. This gave Sarah additional time to compose herself, and by the time the duke appeared, she was ready for him.

Which is not to say the mode of his arrival did not surprise her, for though now immaculately groomed and dressed for dinner, he strode impetuously into the room, exclaiming, "My lady, your library is truly magnificent. I dared not hope—"

Abruptly, he broke off, his eyes widening as they discovered Sarah.

She met his gaze with tolerant amusement.

He recovered quickly. "My fair unknown!" He smiled and bowed before turning to Lady Whitmore. "Forgive me, ma'am, I did not realize you had other guests. My enthusiasm ran away with me."

"So we perceive," Lady Whitmore replied pleasantly. "Allow me to present Miss Sarah and Miss Hammy. Ladies, His Grace, the Duke of Vexen. And Mr. James."

Only then did Sarah notice the gentleman who had followed the duke. A quiet, self-effacing man, perhaps a secretary or assistant of some kind. Possibly the same man who had accompanied him across the courtyard, though she wondered how huge an entourage he traveled with. But she could not allow her mind to wander while he was bearing down upon her.

She could not help the flutter of her heart, for with the teasing smile in his eyes, he was extremely attractive. But she had herself well in control, offering him her hand with perfect grace.

He took it and bowed over it punctiliously. "Merely Miss Sarah?"

"Merely?" she repeated. "I might accuse you of incivility."

He smiled. "Except you are hardly obtuse and quite understand I meant your lack of surname."

"Most here do not use their surnames," Lady

Whitmore observed. "In Whitmore, people prefer the arts and learning to worldly ambition, and are generally happy to leave high or low rank behind them."

"And yet you have a vast library of genealogy," the duke observed.

"It is the privilege of the Lady of Whitmore," she replied. "I alone know who everyone is."

"But everyone seems to know who *I* am. I feel at a disadvantage."

"Not at all," Sarah assured hm. "Here, no one cares who you are."

He blinked, clearly stunned, and then, to her surprise, let out a breath of laughter. "Well, that will be good for my self-conceit."

"Probably," Sarah agreed serenely. "But you must not mind if you are not intellectually inclined. There are interests and activities to please all tastes."

The duke, who was considered expert in many fields including art, antiquities, and music, swallowed that with a mere quirk of the lips. He sat in the chair next to Sarah's. "I already gather your tastes lie in music. If Fernando Arcadi is your teacher, I am in awe. How did you meet him?"

"Lady Whitmore introduced us. I, too, was in awe, for I had heard him sing in Florence."

"In Florence?" he said quickly. "That is one of my favorite cities in the world."

"And mine…" From there, the time flew as they compared impressions of Florence's art and architecture, moved on to Paris and the Louvre, to Napoleon Bonaparte and the politics of peace in Europe. He had opinions on everything, but seemed eager to hear her views and delighted with her knowledge.

Although she had set out to display these things to him, her pleasure in his approval was tempered by cynicism. She was showing him what a perfect duchess she could be, and part of her tried to despise him for swallowing it.

Even so, she was slightly piqued when he excused himself and gave up his place to Mr. James, going instead to sit by Hammy. To Sarah's indignant gaze, he seemed just as interested in her old governess as in her. Was it all civil pretense?

"You are a friend of His Grace?" she asked Mr. James rather abruptly.

"He is gracious enough to call me so, but in fact, I am employed as his secretary."

"And what are the duties of such a great nobleman's secretary?"

"Whatever he requires. I answer impersonal correspondence, help with speeches he chooses to make in the House of Lords, catalogue his library and his collections…"

"What sort of collections?"

"Art, rare books and manuscripts, all kinds of

artifacts and antiquities from all over the world, including Egypt and the Americas. He travels a great deal."

"And what brings him to Whitmore?"

Mr. James smiled. "Vikings."

It certainly gave her something to tease him with when she was, inevitably, placed beside him at dinner.

"It is odd," she observed, setting down her soup spoon. "You do not *look* like a man who dreams of murder and pillage."

He blinked. "Then I am happy to inform you appearance does not lie. Why should you imagine such violence appeals to me?"

"Vikings," she said innocently.

To her surprise, he laughed. "You have been talking to Mr. James. But the Norsemen were much more interesting people than you might imagine. Fierce warriors, it is true, but also farmers and great craftsmen. We have found several beautiful items in Ireland that I believe to be the work of Norse settlers there. I'm sure there must be similar artifacts buried along this coast."

"What sort of items?"

"Several broaches, used for fastening cloaks, some weapons, and a very fine necklace." He smiled, and his gaze dropped to her throat. "It would look charming on you. A blending of barbaric and refined beauty,"

"Hmm. Which refers to me?"

His brows lifted. "Both."

For an instant, she feared he had recognized her, for at sixteen she had indeed been a little barbarian, though not very beautiful.

"I'm sure I should feel insulted to be called barbaric," she managed.

"Trust me, it detracts nothing from your beauty. But it's there in your eyes, just occasionally. Warning me, perhaps, not to stray beyond the line."

"You must be mistaken, sir," she retorted. "What do I have to fear from so perfect a gentleman as the Duke of Vexen?"

"I was about to ask you the same question."

She picked up her wine glass and sipped. "If you imagine I am afraid, sir, I can only assume the flaw is yours."

"That goes without saying." He smiled. "I *am* flawed. I cannot help pursuing beauty."

"For your collection? Why, sir, now who is barbaric?"

He laughed with what sounded like genuine delight, and she smiled to have drawn the noose of his downfall just a little tighter.

>>>><<<<

OH, YES, SHE intrigued him. She was never short of a clever riposte. Her conversation was witty, her opinions well-informed, her knowledge far greater than most young women of her age and class. She moved with an unconscious grace that inflamed him. Her beauty snatched at his breath. And yet, none of that explained the sheer intensity of his attraction.

Something about her still tugged at his memory, though if he had met her before, surely, he could not have forgotten. Perhaps his sense of familiarity lay merely in the fact that he liked her. A woman who could be a friend... Now there was a novelty. The women in his life to date had all proved to be grasping, wanting always more money and gifts. Or—worse—to marry him and be a duchess.

Miss Sarah, he knew instinctively, was too honest for such tricks. He was not even sure she liked him very much. Well, he thought, as he and James strolled along the wide hall to rejoin the ladies in the drawing room, he had some time to win her over, if he was to begin work on this possible burial site.

As a result, he did not go straight to her, but chose a seat beside his hostess to compliment her on the fineness of her food and wine.

"Thank you. My cook and my wine are both of excellent vintage," Lady Whitmore quipped. "As am I."

He laughed, noticing with irritation that Sarah smiled up at James. He wondered how generous he would feel should she prefer his secretary to him.

"I see you have noticed my protégée," Lady Whitmore observed.

"Who would not? She is as beautiful as she is charming."

"Isn't she? And delightfully accomplished."

His gaze came back to Lady Whitmore. "Accomplished? Meaning she is a lady and not a professional performer? I had gathered as much."

She nodded. "Then I know I may count on you to act accordingly as a gentleman."

He allowed a hint of haughtiness into his expression. "I trust you have never heard I acted in any other way."

To his surprise, his rebuke only softened her eyes. "Why, how like your father you are."

He blinked. "You knew my father?"

"In a different age, a different life."

"Then it is for his sake you give me permission to dig?"

"Oh, no. Merely my own curiosity."

Exactly what kind of digging she referred to could be taken one of two ways at the moment— dig into the details of her past and find what kind of relationship she had with his father or the archaeological type. He smiled warmly at her, liking her more each time he talked with her.

In fact, his whole experience at Whitmore had been rather pleasant. And not just because of his hostess or even the beautiful Sarah—there was something charming, almost magical about this place. Maybe the salt air and sea settled him more than he knew. Or perhaps he had visited this part of the country as a boy and simply did not recall it. Regardless, a comforting familiarity had settled about him since his arrival—even his sleep had improved.

"Where did your thoughts wander to just now?" she asked.

"Excuse me?" He snapped back to the present.

"You seemed preoccupied with something of importance, Your Grace," Lady Whitmore observed. "I must apologize, I am an overly curious type."

"There is no need for apology. I feel as if I have been here before, perhaps met you or even Miss Sarah."

Once again, his hostess's expression softened, sadness in her eyes. "You would not be the first to claim such a thing. Whitmore is a special place to all who visit, I think."

He nodded. "The air is superb, and the women..." He glanced toward Sarah, then back to Lady Whitmore. "Beautiful."

"You are flattering us, Your Grace."

"No, I am not the sort to pay a compliment where it is not deserved. I can honestly say, I almost envy your informal life here. It appeals to me more than you know."

She placed her right hand over her heart. "Please know, you are welcome to stay here as long as you wish."

"I deeply appreciate your hospitality, Lady Whitmore. And I may very well accept your offer until I can find a suitable place to purchase in the area."

She looked surprised by his declaration. "You wish to buy land here?"

"I wish to buy a small estate if there is one to be had."

She cleared her throat, almost struggling to find words. "I own most of the land and cottages around Whitmore, even the village. But there are farms and several minor estates to the west and north of the village."

"Perhaps once the exhibition is over, we could find the time to discuss the possibility of you selling some of that land to me?"

Before Lady Whitmore could answer, the double doors to the drawing room were rudely thrown open, and Signor Arcadi swept into the room, followed by several servants looking horrified.

"Forgive me, Madam..." the butler began, but his mistress patted his arm affectionately.

"It is not your fault—no one can control Arcadi, no one."

"Do I require a leash, Lady Whitmore?" the

arrogant man asked, staring at her. "I find my schedule has been completely undone. How can I possibly train a future..." He halted and his eyes narrowed on Leonard. "There...the very cause of my fury!"

Leonard took a deep breath, knowing he must handle the celebrated artist with care. However, he would not tolerate disrespect of any kind, not toward himself or Lady Whitmore. "Signor Arcadi, how may I assist you?"

"That is a dangerous question, sir!"

Leonard chuckled lightly. "It is a simple question that you are free to answer without reprisal."

The man smirked. "Leave this house. In fact, leave Whitmore. That would satisfy me and return balance to my life." He crossed his arms over his chest, waiting for the duke's reply.

"Signor Arcadi," Lady Whitmore sat up, her shoulders suddenly tense. "The Duke of Vexen is an honored guest and will be going nowhere. I insist you learn to get along with my guests or perhaps I will have to..."

The artist threw his hands up, turned his attention to Miss Sarah and Mr. James, and then stalked over to where they sat together. "It seems I cannot take my eyes off of you!"

"Whatever do you mean?" Sarah asked, obviously upset by the tone Arcadi had taken with her.

"First the duke, and now this man. Are you here to sing, Miss Sarah, or to snare a husband?"

Leonard gritted his teeth, moving closer to the edge of the settee.

"No." Lady Whitmore squeezed his hand. "Let this play out naturally, please."

With a nod of compliance, he tried to relax again.

"That is an impertinent question," Sarah said. "After all the weeks I have spent with you preparing for tomorrow, I would think..."

Arcadi clapped his hands loudly, interrupting her. "Then you shall sing!" he commanded.

"Yes, I know, tomorrow evening."

"No." He pointed at the pianoforte in the corner of the well-appointed drawing room. "Now." He stormed over to it, pulled the bench out, and dropped onto the cushioned seat, cracking his knuckles and positioning his fingers over the keys.

The moment his fingertips made contact with the instrument, the heavy mood in the room lifted, and poetry of sound, soothing and hauntingly beautiful, tamed the beast inside Leonard. He looked about the room, noticing the same effect it had on everyone. That was why such an ill-tempered man would be tolerated in any setting, his talent overshadowed his poor manners.

Even Sarah had seemed to be transformed,

her features serene as she approached the pianoforte, though Leonard swore her hands were trembling as she clasped them in front of her.

"What will she sing for us?" he whispered to Lady Whitmore.

"I am sure one of the pieces selected for her performance tomorrow."

"One would think her master would wish her to rest the night before such an important event."

"One would think," she agreed as she gazed in the direction of Sarah.

The music lightened, and Sarah opened her delectable mouth, and the first line of *Robin Adair* lit the duke on fire with admiration and lust. Miss Sarah could charm the paper off the walls if she so chose.

Upon singing the second chorus of the beloved song, something swift and painful slammed Leonard in the chest. Realization... What a fool he had been, blinded by feminine beauty, outwitted by a girl who had once thrown apples at him, smacking not only his carriage, but his head—several times. This time, he could not control himself and shot up from the settee, suddenly an empowered predator, lurking along the perimeter of the room.

Miss Sarah could not hide her true identity from him any longer! And Lady Whitmore must know it, for she had gasped when he left his seat with such force. Yes, that hoyden could dress herself up in silk gowns and walk with grace as any fine lady would, but those eyes, that almost crooked smile that made her more tempting than any woman he had ever seen before, gave her away.

To think he had almost offered for her when she was still climbing trees like a wild lad. Yes, he had been amused by her unbridled ways, but she would never be a duchess, that's what he had thought then, but now?

He stopped just a few feet from her, gaze roaming freely over her as she sang, her dark hair hanging in loose curls down her back, her powder-blue gown demurely cut to fit her curves but not reveal what was underneath. He breathed in her lavender perfume, loosening his cravat just a hint so he could swallow more easily. She didn't just cause his pantaloons to tighten, his throat and heart squeezed at him, too!

Damn fate for throwing them together this way. It would have been better if he had never met up with her again, for he had heard how disappointed she had been when he had refused the match those two long years ago. Though he had not refused the girl outright, he had preferred to find a mature woman to take as wife.

He found himself smiling so hard it hurt.

"Your Grace," he heard Sarah call.

"Yes?" His eyes had never left her, but his

thoughts had wandered into the past.

"The song has finished, yet you are staring at me, almost through me."

The duke searched for Arcadi, but the man was nowhere to be found. "Your master?"

She rolled her eyes. "He is my teacher, sir."

Yes. "And quite taken with you, I think," Leonard said.

Her eyes widened. "Y-you think Signor Arcadi is in love with me?"

Jealously pricked Leonard. "I do not recall saying love, Miss Sarah." Leonard knew Arcadi's reputation with women across the continent.

"Yes, you said taken with me."

"That can mean many things."

"Oh?" She tilted her head and met his gaze. "As you seem taken with me, Your Grace?"

There she was—the brazen girl in the tree! "I will not deny it," he said, almost challenging her. "But I could say the same about you."

Her mouth opened and closed again, obviously shocked by his words. "But I hardly know you."

He took a step closer, and she let out a heavy sigh. "Does it not feel as if we have met before?"

"No," she rejected immediately. "I have been here for over a year, closed off from Society. Where would we have met, sir? London?"

"Yes."

"Perhaps I remind you of someone."

He laughed, and she shuffled on her feet. "Suddenly I find myself hungry for more of Lady Whitmore's apple tarts. Would you care to join me, Miss Sarah?" His jesting would stop now, for he did not wish to make her so uncomfortable that she would refuse to perform tomorrow. But once the exhibition was over, he would have his moment with her—for she knew exactly who he was. And he wanted her—for just what he didn't know at the moment, but it must begin with a kiss.

Those sweet lips, currently pursed with distaste, should be kissed every day, and only by him.

SARAH WOKE THE following morning with a knot of excitement in her stomach. And not a little unease caused by Arcadi's outburst.

She lay for a little, mulling things over. For the first time it struck her that she was not being fair to Arcadi. He had no idea of her birth and clearly assumed he was training her for the stage, instead of the drawing room.

Oh well, it might yet come to the stage if my parents cast me off. For more than a year, she had thought no further than enslaving and rejecting the duke. And delivering a lesson to her parents.

But she had to admit the journey had become a pleasure in itself, and her future was unclear. *Whatever it holds, I will enjoy it. Secure in the knowledge that I have dealt most justly with Vexen's slights.*

On the other hand, her victory over the duke was not assured. He was...unpredictable, as his strange reaction to Arcadi's outburst showed. At one moment, he was clearly intrigued, elegantly flirting. The next, he had charged upon her almost like an untamed animal. She forgave his temper, since it appeared to spring from jealousy, but the incident had given her a taste of a whole new side of him—raw and passionate and ungoverned by society's rules.

A little shiver of excitement ran down her spine. It came to her that she was playing with fire. Poking a lion...

Enough of this silliness! She threw off the covers and went to call to the maid for bath water. She meant to look and feel at her best today.

Accordingly, she donned her new day gown of jonquil yellow, trimmed with white lace, and a very fetching hat with a matching dyed yellow feather, which she wore at a jaunty angle. They had been made in Whitmore's workshops, but looked at least as good as the best London or even Paris had to offer. And, as she and Hammy entered the crowded assembly rooms, she was aware that several heads turned in their direction and lingered. She did not deign to respond to vulgar stares, merely greeted acquaintances as they made their way through the gallery.

It seemed there were many visitors to Whitmore for the event, including several members of the *ton* whom she recognized from their visits to her parents' home. Of course, they did not recognize her, and she pretended not to know them.

But among one group of fashionable strangers, she spotted the Duke of Vexen, his head slightly bent to listen to the beautiful woman beside him. Despite his expression of interest, his gaze lifted and met hers.

He inclined his head. So did she, and passed on toward her friend, an accomplished poet who called herself Miss Smith.

"That's a dashed beautiful girl," she overheard one of his companions observe, a shade too loudly for discretion. "You might arrange an introduction, Duke."

"I might," he agreed, and she heard no more.

A bell tinkled, quieting the crowd, and everyone, including Sarah, turned to face the little platform. The duke stepped nimbly up, accepting the glass of champagne handed to him. Liveried servants with trays of glasses passed among the crowd as Vexen began to speak.

"It falls to me to welcome you to Whitmore, on behalf of the gracious Lady Whitmore, who has made this day possible."

Sarah glanced around, but as usual among visitors, her ladyship was nowhere to be seen.

"To be honest," the duke said humorously, "I always meant to announce that it was my pleasure to open this exhibition. But I did not expect to mean it to quite this degree. You will find, as I did, an astonishing array of fresh talent, beauty, and skill in this room, so please, take the time to truly look at the work on display. You will find it well worth your time—and money, though I shall do my best to outbid you! I give you a toast—to the art of Whitmore."

His speech surprised Sarah by its simplicity and appreciation. There was no effort to show off among his fine friends or to detract from the artists by his own wit. And what His Grace had endorsed, the rest were eager to view.

Sarah, examining a delightful sculpture between Hammy and Miss Smith, knew a flutter of anticipation as she saw Vexen making his way slowly but inexorably toward them. The fashionable lady she had already noticed drew his attention to the painting she was examining. He smiled and said a few words, but kept walking. Hastily. Sarah returned her attention to the sculpture of a child with a mischievous smile.

"I imagine you were exactly like that," Miss Smith remarked.

"She was," Hammy confirmed.

"She was what?" the duke asked mildly. "Good afternoon, ladies.

"A mischievous child," Miss Smith explained when the introductions had been made. "Exactly like this charming sculpture."

Vexen regarded it critically and then looked Sarah over in much the same manner, a half-smile lurking on his lips. "They are both charming, certainly, though Miss Sarah has the advantage in beauty, and I cannot imagine she was ever as naughty as this child."

"Hah!" Hammy exclaimed.

"Why," the duke continued, returning his attention to the sculpture, "this child looks as if he could get up to anything, even throw fruit at one's back in passing, just to test his aim. Acquit Miss Sarah of such imprudence."

"Of course, I acquit her of it *now*," Hammy said.

"In that case, I feel brave enough to offer my escort," the duke replied, smiling.

Sarah smiled back in polite acceptance, but his words inspired a twinge of unease. *Why would he think of throwing fruit at someone?*

Because it had happened to him…

And now that she thought of it, in the strange interlude after Arcadi's invasion and her song, had he not mentioned apple tarts?

Yes, but there *were* apple tarts, and she was being silly, examining everything through her own guilt.

Even though I am not guilty. He *is…*

Tea was served in the music room, where chairs and tables had been set out. Inevitably, as people mingled and Sarah was joined by old Whitmore friends, Vexen and she were separated. Although she was eager to look around and see if he watched her, she controlled herself, and in time was rewarded by his return, along with the fashionable lady and the gentleman who had called her beautiful.

Vexen performed the introductions. The newcomers were a Mr. Shaddleton and his sister Lady Loxley, who looked thoroughly amused by the names presented to her.

However, to Sarah's surprise, Miss Loxley sat down next to her and smiled. "So, have you lived for long in Whitmore?"

"A little over a year."

"And is one of those charming paintings yours, perhaps?"

"Oh, no," Sarah replied. "I am not nearly good enough for such recognition."

"No? But you do study accomplishments here? What is your favorite?"

"Singing."

"Ah." Lady Loxley smiled. "Perhaps you are involved in tonight's musical evening?"

"I do have that honor," Saraah admitted, and could have sworn an expression of annoyed surprise flashed through the other woman's eyes.

However, at least she held her smile. "Then I can see why His Grace wishes to stay longer. He is devoted to music. Which is one reason he and I suit so well."

Sarah hid the pained catching of her breath. "And does your husband also enjoy music?"

"He did when he was alive," Lady Loxley drawled.

"Forgive me, I did not know," Sarah said awkwardly. "I'm sorry if I caused you pain."

Lady Loxley waved a careless hand. "Not at all. I have grown used to the advantages of widowhood." She smiled, her gaze flitting to the duke.

So, was Sarah meant to understand that Vexen and Lady Loxley were engaged? Or merely lovers? Either made no difference. That the older woman was subtly warning her off was in fact a triumph for Sarah, because Lady Loxley clearly felt her position threatened.

Well you may have him, Sarah thought contemptuously. *When I am done.*

"You have not got your tea yet," Vexen noted to his friends. "Let us move to a different table so that we do not cramp these ladies."

Lady Loxley smiled. "Afraid we'll swap secrets about you, my lord duke?"

Sarah had never seen anyone's eyes grow so icy so quickly. It was almost frightening. "No," he drawled, holding Lady Loxley's chair, "for the simple reason neither of you knows any."

Sarah could only be relieved when he took them away. For once, it seemed to be someone else who had committed the cardinal sin of vulgarity.

Only as she and Hammy left the assembly rooms did she speak to him again. Most of the ladies were leaving, as the gentlemen were about to begin an auction for the works of art. But Vexen stood outside, gazing through a gap in the cottages toward the sea. He looked dark and brooding and extraordinarily handsome.

But he glanced round at their approach and smiled spontaneously as he walked toward them. "Would you like me to buy any items for you?"

"Thank you, no," Sarah replied firmly.

"But you will return for the banquet?"

Was that a trace of anxiety in his voice? Was he actually afraid Lady Loxley's unsubtle hints had upset her? "Of course," she replied.

"Then may I take you in, Miss Sarah?"

"I believe the seating is already arranged. But if we do not meet at dinner, I'm sure we'll meet later in the music room."

"I shall make certain of it." His eyes bored into hers with intensity. Then, with a flickering smile, he bowed and strode back inside the assembly rooms.

"I HAVE GIVEN her many chances to understand that I know who she is, Mr. James, but for some reason, perhaps fear or mere stubbornness, Miss Sarah refuses to acknowledge me, to admit we were nearly engaged two years ago."

Mr. James chuckled and blew out a smoke ring from the cigar in his hand. "Did it ever occur to you, Your Grace, that she is playing a bit of cat and mouse with you?"

Leonard's brow arched in question. "She is too young to be that jaded, Mr. James."

His secretary obviously disagreed, for his mouth tightened before he spoke again. "I have been with you for six years, sir. And I recall the very moment you returned from meeting her—how disappointed you were that she was not ready for marriage. You had struggled with the idea of marriage in general, but once you identified Miss Sarah as a perfect match through her father, your doubts eased, I believe."

"Indeed, they did." He would not deny the range of emotions he experienced when he climbed into his carriage and traveled to meet his soon-to-be bride. The anticipation, the hope she would suit him... It had all been undone by apples and a gloriously mischievous child in a tree. He grinned.

"Ah," Mr. James said. "You are fond of the memory, then?"

"I appreciate it, for it has brought me to this moment, has it not?"

Mr. James nodded.

"How often do you get a second chance, Mr. James?"

Just then, the French doors opened, and Lady Whitmore and her companion joined them. "I am sorry to intrude, Your Grace, Mr. James," she said. "But the moment to announce the winners of the silent auction has arrived. As my guest of honor, the pieces you have won will be shared first. It gives me great pleasure to inform you that the sculpture you wanted, the one with the mother and child, is most certainly yours. You outdid the closest bidder by a hundred pounds!"

"Well…"

"I believe you are aware that some of the proceeds raised tonight are donated to the Whitmore Fund that supports underprivileged young ladies in need of education."

"I will not deny it, Lady Whitmore. I like what you do here."

She tapped him on the shoulder with her fan. "You are certainly full of surprises, Your Grace."

Leonard bowed respectfully, that odd sensation that he had met this lady before making the hairs on the back of his neck stand on end. When he raised his head, he found her gazing at him—

her blue eyes filled with warmth and sadness. It pained him to think this gracious woman harbored pain inside her heart.

"Shall we?" He offered his arm to Lady Whitmore, and Mr, James did the same with her companion.

As they entered the main assembly room, the crowd parted and applause sounded.

Leonard found himself on the stage with Lady Whitmore, the adulation from the people very real for the fine woman standing at his side. Once the noise settled, she stepped forward.

"Thank you all for attending the art exhibition. I am proud to say that every piece sold. As you know, Whitmore is *sui generis*, there is no other place like it in England. We welcome all, great and small, accomplished or not, in hope that everyone can find happiness in an era of turbulence and war."

The crowd broke into applause again.

Lady Whitmore raised her hand to silence them.

"We certainly welcome new friends." She turned to the duke. "I believe His Grace, the Duke of Vexen, will have a substantial role in the future of Whitmore."

Leonard smiled, only a bit uncomfortable with the attention. If it were London, he would have walked off the stage. He truly disliked attention of any kind, but for some reason, this felt right.

"And now, Sir Roger will happily announce our winners. Please join us for dinner, after."

Once his prizes were announced, including the sculpture that reminded him of Sarah when he first met her and three paintings, he joined Lady Whitmore, her companion, and Mr. James again.

"You see," Lady Whitmore said, "it was well worth coming here, was it not?" She moved aside, giving Leonard a clear view of the entrance to the assembly rooms.

Dressed in a gown the shimmering color of moonlight, her hair swept up, revealing lovely shoulders and a neck meant for kissing, Sarah, elegant and almost understated, stepped into the room. A diamond and gold necklace adorned her throat, and Leonard's heart thundered with desire—perilous and uncontainable. His hand actually shook with need as he let his arms fall to his sides, his penetrating gaze undressing her layer by layer.

Mr. James tapped him on the back and whispered, "Your intentions are showing, sir."

Perhaps he should just rip his heart out now and offer it to her. For no matter what he did at this point, he wanted her.

UNFORTUNATELY, SARAH DID not have the pleasure of being seated next to the Duke of Vexen at dinner. However, he was within sight and did not hide his interest in her, nor look away whenever their gazes met.

She had been placed between a young lord, the Earl of Trenton, and an elderly widow, Lady Billows. The conversation, just as the food, was pleasant and diverting.

"Your singing capabilities have been praised by many here this evening, Miss Sarah," the earl said to her, not hiding his attraction but doing so within the boundaries of respectability. "If your voice is as lovely as you are, I am sure you will be a marvelous success."

Sarah smiled and sipped her wine, already nervous. Her performance was only two hours away, and the butterflies in her stomach only increased. "I could not say, my lord, but hope my devotion to training with Signor Arcadi will be rewarded with his approval tonight."

"What a charming young woman you are," Lady Billows said. "Showing confidence in your accomplishments is not considered vanity, my dear."

Sarah turned to her with a smile. "Thank you, Lady Billows. Are you fond of music?"

"I am a patron of the arts, much like our esteemed guest of honor, the Duke of Vexen. Not to mention Lady Whitmore's dedication to charitable events is unmatched from here to London."

"You are close friends with our hostess, then?" Sarah asked.

"I am indeed. We are old friends, used to spend summers together..." She suddenly stopped herself. "You must excuse me. I have said too much already."

"Too much?"

"Of course the rules would be unknown to you, this is your first event at Whitmore, is it not?"

"Yes, it is."

"Those invited to the events are permitted to use their full names," the earl said, drawing her attention back to him. "But Lady Whitmore's students, whether highborn or not, are to remain anonymous. That is why we haven't questioned you about your name or family."

"I knew this, but did not think it extended to the guests quite so severely."

"How else would our hostess reach such levels of respectability and success?" Lady Billows asked. "All of the *ton* are not welcome here, as some would never be able to keep quiet about what goes on. Even the gossip sheets have failed to infiltrate Whitmore."

Sarah swallowed down her building concern that her family, the duke, or possibly even one of the guests present would deduce who she was and why she had come here. Reaching for a dessert fork, she tasted the lemon tart, which melted in her mouth. She had been careful to eat only tiny portions so she would not be incapable of performing. Too much food and wine could definitely affect her voice.

"How many events have you attended here, Lady Billows?"

"Twenty or so, I believe. Most are not as elaborate as this, but just as enjoyable."

"And you, sir?"

"This is my third year to support Lady Whitmore's mission."

"Mission?" Sarah asked, surprised by his choice of words.

"Yes, mission is the perfect word for what she intends," the earl said. "To provide a means for people often forgotten to find a way to support themselves. It is not a unique idea, but her approach to accomplishing it is."

"I am humbled by your support for Lady Whitmore and your enthusiasm to help underprivileged women."

He shrugged. "I have three sisters, Miss Sarah—one of them close in age to you, I believe. If she were ever to..." He quickly took up his wine glass and swallowed it down, appearing to grow uncomfortable.

"I did not mean to unsettle you, my lord."

"You didn't. I'm afraid I have a soft spot for

my siblings, each of them strong-willed and independent. Johanna, the eldest, is just eighteen. Miriam is sixteen, and Regina, thirteen."

"Do you have siblings, Miss Sarah?" he asked.

"I am afraid I cannot answer questions of such a personal nature."

"You see," Lady Billows said with an approving tone, "you are learning quickly."

"Were you testing me, sir?"

The earl met her gaze. "In a way. But you intrigue me, Miss Sarah, I will not lie. Perhaps I may call on you when you are next in London."

Lady Billows gave a feminine cough. "My dear, you mustn't prey upon the young lady right before her performance!"

"My intentions are honorable," he said to Lady Billows, then reached for Sarah's hand and patted it.

She gaped at him for a moment, then gently withdrew her hand, shocked that she wasn't offended by his public gesture of affection. Only…

She gazed in the direction of the Duke of Vexen, finding his green eyes intently watching her, his expression severe.

Lady Billows leaned close to her. "You seem to have two very serious admirers, my dear. Tread carefully, for both of these men are powerful, influential, and wealthy. Do not trifle with either one. And if neither appeal to you, make it known right away. A good reputation is the most important thing any young lady has."

Sarah nodded. "Thank you for your advice, Lady Billows."

"And Lady Sarah," she said, causing Sarah to nearly fall out of her chair. "Your father and mother miss you very much."

Sarah promptly folded her linen napkin and placed it on the table, stood slowly, and excused herself from the room.

HE COULD NOT, would not, stay seated for the duration of Sarah's performance. The first two songs were enough to convince him she could make angels weep, and even more evident, she could bring an earl to his knees.

Making his way to the back of the room, he left unnoticed, everyone enthralled by her flawless voice. A siren meant to torment him, though he had no real claim on her.

The main room was nearly empty; staff were busy cleaning up. He found a cushioned bench in a corner and sat down, the weight of the world suddenly on his shoulders. Tonight must not be wasted; he would have a private moment with Sarah and convince her to acknowledge him.

To the devil!

Another man should not be holding her hand, touching her in any way.

He breathed in deeply and closed his eyes, taking in the words she sang, the tone of her voice, imagining her pretty features, her dark hair and eyes imprinted on his mind forever.

Could anyone blame him for not extending an offer of marriage to her before? A duchess who climbed trees and ran about like a lad? She would have slid down every banister inside his townhouse to the shock and disapproval of his staff, perhaps even wear pantaloons! *Christ in heaven.*

The singing stopped, and there was a long moment of silence, and Leonard jumped to his feet. Did they not appreciate her extraordinary talent? He must go to her immediately... After taking only two steps, the room exploded with applause. Miss Sarah, his Lady Sarah, was a success.

Reclaiming his seat, he realized it would be a long wait before the crowd dispersed and gave him a chance to speak with her.

"She is everything we had hoped for." Lady Whitmore appeared from nowhere.

He looked up, her rose-colored gown and matching feathers in her hair complemented her exceedingly well. "Your musicale is a success."

"It is not for me, Your Grace. This was for the artists and Sarah to showcase their talents. I am a means to an end, nothing more."

"You are a savior to these young ladies, believe me."

"Do you need saving, Your Grace?"

She seemed suddenly serious.

"I am blessed with good health and a joyous life, Lady Whitmore."

"But have not found love yet."

"There was a time…"

She nodded in understanding and sat beside him. "It is my duty to know things."

"What kind of things?" Another mystery about this fascinating woman.

"Secrets, connections, and perhaps even regrets of the women who live with me."

"And the men who visit?"

Her eyes lit up. "Ah, yes, that, too."

"You are not going to blackmail me, are you, Lady Whitmore?"

She chuckled so deeply, he could not help but smile.

"Of course not. Have you done something so bad that one could attempt to?"

"Not that I recall."

She rolled her eyes and touched his hand. "You are part rogue, I believe."

"I am a gentleman through and through."

"I believe you," she said. "But now let us discuss Miss Sarah."

"I would rather not."

"Why? Because you are smitten with her?"

He turned to her, unable to deny anything. "If you are such a mistress of knowledge—secrets…"

"Then I should know that you have a prior acquaintance with Miss Sarah and know exactly who she is?"

If Lady Whitmore was trying to impress him, she had. "Yes."

"Why did you not reveal this to anyone?" she asked.

"What purpose would that have served? If she wishes to remain anonymous, there must be good reason. Though I intend on finding that out tonight."

"That is fair enough," she said. "But I warn you, she is inexperienced and deeply wounded by past events."

"What events?"

She shook her head. "It is not my place to say. But out of respect and affection for you, I wanted to give you that bit of information. What she thinks she wants is not what she really needs."

Leonard would not press her for more information. Though to his vast irritation, he had a rival now, one he rather liked before tonight.

"Do not worry about the Earl of Trenton."

"Madame?"

"After everything we've discussed tonight,

you would try and deny you are jealous he sat with her at dinner?"

Leonard stood and grinned down at her. "You are a spitfire, Lady Whitmore, one to be feared."

She rose, amused by his compliment. "You and Miss Sarah are long overdue for a reunion. I wish you luck."

FINALLY, AFTER THREE hours of waiting, the last of the crowd filtered out of the assembly rooms, leaving Sarah with her teacher. The doors to the room were open, and Leonard could hear them talking.

"You were magnificent, Sarah," Signor Arcadi said. "This is only the beginning of your career—I am prepared to travel with you across Europe, where you will become famous, possibly sing for kings and queens."

"I-I am humbled by your praise, Signor Arcadi," Sarah stuttered. "But I have never intended to seek fame or leave England."

"No?" The teacher's voice went up and octave, anger seeping into his tone. "Then why have I wasted a year of my life? To teach a little girl how to sing in drawing rooms for the most passionless audiences I have ever seen?"

"Are you accusing the British of being passionless, sir? I assure you, you could not be more wrong."

"Hush!" he said. "What do you know of such things? You are an innocent."

"I am not unfamiliar with what you refer to. And to my knowledge, Lady Whitmore has paid you handsomely for your services."

"The lady is generous to a fault," Arcadi said. "Though I have nothing bad to say about her, I am ready to leave this village. Come with me, Sarah, if not as my protégée, then as my…"

The Duke of Vexen leaned against the door frame and shook his head admonishingly. "Do not think to finish the thought, sir," he warned.

Arcadi glanced at Leonard, his mouth twisting into a scowl. "Is that a threat, Duke of Vexation?"

Leonard let out a sarcastic laugh, stepping into the space. Arcadi was using his position of trust to take advantage of Sarah, though she had done a fine job of defending herself and her country.

"Is that the best you have, Arcadi? My Eton brothers exhausted that name upon completion of my first year of school."

Arcadi's cheeks turned red as he stared at Sarah. "Secret lovers? Is that the reason for your rejection of my proposal?"

The duke suddenly didn't like the man and

surged forward, grabbing a handful of his collar.
"Perhaps men speak to women that way in Italy,
but here, we refrain from such talk when a lady is
present." He dragged the teacher from the music
room and to the entryway of the assembly
rooms. "If you require an escort home, I will be
happy to accommodate you."

"You are a bastard," Arcadi spat at him before
letting out a huff of rage and stalking away.

Leonard watched him walk down the deserted street, happy he had...

"Your Grace..."

He turned to find a teary-eyed Sarah standing
behind him.

"Are you hurt?" he asked.

"Only my pride."

"Well." He offered his arm and she reluctantly took it. "I think a glass of port might benefit
you greatly."

"Port?"

"Yes."

"What if someone sees me?"

Leonard looked about the room. "Only staff
remain, and from what I am told, they would
never gossip about anyone. They have their own
secrets to keep hidden. Lady Whitmore is
enjoying a comfortable gossip with Miss Hammy.
I believe they will wait for you."

She nodded and let him escort her to the
comfortable library he had been shown earlier. It

boasted leather chairs, shelves filled with leather-bound books, a billiard table, and a private balcony through a set of French doors. She waited by a window while the duke searched for glasses and the much-needed wine. He found it in a cabinet and poured two equal portions and then went to her.

"Come," he said, pressing the crystal glass into her hands, then opening the doors for her. "Fresh air will clear your mind."

"Signor Arcadi says the nighttime air can cause lasting damage to my vocal cords."

"Your teacher is no longer here, Miss Sarah. It is your choice alone now."

She hesitated, as he expected she would, then braved a step outside, pleasing him very much.

She took several small sips of the port, stunned at first by the strong taste. "This is a-a…"

"An acquired taste, perhaps?" He smiled at her.

"Yes. But after taking a few sips, I can feel it warming me to the core."

"Liquid courage has driven many a man to do things he never would have considered while sober."

"Liquid courage?" She giggled sweetly at that. "And a few women, I am sure."

"That, too," he agreed.

"Thank you," she said, turning away to stare down at the garden below. "You defended my honor."

"No gratitude is necessary," he said. "I would come to the aid of any woman."

"Would you?" She turned back to him, the glass in her hand empty.

"Yes," he reassured her, blood boiling for her again. "But especially for you, Lady Sarah."

Jolted by his words, she dropped the glass, and it shattered.

He set his glass on a nearby table and rushed to her, holding her by the arms. "Why did you hide yourself from me?" He gave her a gentle shake.

She met his gaze, the fathomless depths of her dark eyes pulling him in, inviting him to get lost in the windows to her soul. "You rejected me, Your Grace."

"No," he said firmly. "I simply put you off. You needed time to mature, to become who you are now."

"You are the inspiration for whom I have become, sir!"

To her credit, she had the spirit of a warrior, never backing down though he towered over her. "Me? How so?"

"You did not wish to ally yourself with a child, according to what my mother told me. You found me lacking in the qualities a future duchess should possess."

A knot formed in his stomach, for he had

never said those things, though he had thought them, and rightly so. "I found you charming and sweet, if not overly mischievous, but very likable, Sarah. I am twenty-eight, and you, if I am correct, are soon to be nineteen. What kind of beast would marry and bed a girl still full of the wonder and energy of a child? I preferred to give you time to grow up."

"No." She shook free of his grasp.

"Yes," he countered. "I would never lie to you."

She hugged herself protectively, glancing up at him. "You climbed that blasted tree, sat next to me, and threw an apple or two, if I recall properly."

"Three," he said.

"Three," she repeated. "You kissed my cheek before you climbed down."

"I did, and still do not regret it, for it has led me here, to this moment."

"What moment?" she inquired.

"This." He pulled her into his arms, slanted his mouth over hers, his arms enveloping her in a strong yet gentle embrace, his lips tracing the curves of her own, his soul breathing in her scent, her warmth, her very essence.

She sighed, leaning into him, her lips parting enough for his tongue to meet hers, their kiss deepening, and her arms locking around his neck, encouraging him to taste her, to hold her.

"Sarah," he whispered, "why did you hide from me?"

"Be quiet, Your Grace," she breathed, "and kiss me more."

His arousal grew to new levels, his excitement more than evident as it pressed into her, but she didn't seem alarmed by it. Her lips were so soft, so pliant, so hungry. And his... Damn him for ever walking away from her, for not honoring the betrothal and simply waiting for her to grow up. This woman, this passionate creature in his arms deserved to be his duchess, his goddess even—but would she accept his offer for marriage?

Then without warning, she pulled away, peering up at him with awe. "Forgive me."

He chuckled and reached for her, but she stepped back. "Whatever for?" He knew there was a dangerous glint in his eyes, there was no hiding his desire, no need to. She obviously felt the same, and it frightened her.

"For misleading you, Your Grace. Our kiss was simply a way for me to put our prior connection in the past—for I have often wondered what would have happened if you had accepted me that day."

Had he heard her correctly? The kiss had meant nothing? He stared at her, confused.

"Good evening, Your Grace," she whispered and left him standing on the balcony alone.

CHAPTER FIVE

B Y THE TIME she closed the library door, her evening's triumphs tasted like ashes. Her social and musical successes were hollow when there was no elation about *this*, the point of it all.

Why does he not follow me?

Not that she wished him to. Truly, she didn't. Her exit had been superb, the expression on his face just as satisfyingly lost as she hoped for.

So why did she not feel better? Where was her sense of justice and victory?

Hurrying downstairs in search of Hammy, it came to her that she had lost.

Lost his friendship, lost hope of any more such devastating kisses… She paused, touching her lips in wonder, and then ran furiously on.

As she had expected, Hammy was in the small ladies' withdrawing room on the ground floor, sitting very close to Lady Whitmore. Both heads snapped around to face her as she burst into the room.

Hastily, she tried to pull her broken pieces together. She dropped a curtsey to her ladyship, but blurted almost immediately, "Hammy, let's go. I am suddenly very tired."

"Of course." Her old governess bounded at once to her feet. "You have had such an exhausting day! We were just saying how proud we were of you."

She tried to smile. She didn't feel worthy of their pride. She felt mean-spirited and cruel. The expression on Vexen's face would surely haunt her forever.

Or perhaps only until she fell asleep.

"Where did you leave His Grace?" Lady Whitmore asked mildly.

Sarah waved one vague hand. "Up in the library, I think."

But her ladyship's eyes held her still. "Perhaps there is something you would like to tell us?"

Sarah shook her head mutely, trying to swallow the sudden lump in her throat.

"I see. You have had your revenge."

"I said I would and I did," Sarah said defiantly.

"Then you had best go home with Miss Hammond."

Why did she feel like a scolded child again? It seemed she had lost Lady Whitmore's good opinion, too, and yet she had told her from the beginning what she intended.

Hammy took her arm and led her away.

In the short walk to the cottage, Sarah was aware of her companion's searching gaze, but neither said anything.

Were it not for Hammy, I would be completely alone. Sarah thrust the thought aside as self-pitying drivel of the kind she most detested. All the same, she hugged her old governess quite fiercely before picking up the bedroom candle and fleeing upstairs to her chamber.

Only there, with the curtains closed, could she cast herself on her bed and weep. For what, she didn't yet know, but whatever happened now, her life had changed once more.

>>>><<<<

LADY WHITMORE FOUND him still on the balcony.

She came and stood beside him. "Your reunion did not prosper."

He let out a short laugh but saw her shiver and immediately offered her his arm. "Come inside, ma'am. The night is too chilly."

She turned with clear relief to walk back into the room and he closed the doors.

"What happened?" she asked bluntly.

His lip curled in self-deprecation. "I wish I

knew. At first, she seemed appalled that I had recognized her, but we talked and she seemed to accept it, accept me. I could have sworn she was not indifferent, and yet… I kissed her."

"Did she like it?"

He dragged his hand over his face and sat down abruptly beside her. "I thought so. And then she pulled away, remarked she had always been curious about me and then walked away. As though it meant nothing. As though *I* meant nothing."

Lady Whitmore sighed and patted his knee. "Poor boy. I don't suppose that happens to you very often. But look at it from her point of view. Is that not exactly what you did to her two years ago? Walked away as if she meant nothing?"

He stared at her, frowning. "She was a child. Would it have been honorable to take her as she was?"

"Forget your honor," Lady Whitmore said impatiently. "Sarah did not consider herself a child. No one does at sixteen. To her, you trifled with her, rejected her, and walked away without a backward glance. It may have been honorable, Your Grace, but it was not kind."

His frown deepened. "And so, she was playing a game," he said slowly. "I tried to end it, and she declared victory. Because I gave her what she wanted,"

"And does that victory stand?" Lady

Whitmore wondered. "Do you surrender to the chit? Out of honor and kindness, of course."

Thoughtfully, he smoothed the fabric of his pantaloons. He glanced up and cast her a lopsided smile. "I don't believe I do. The game does not end until *I* say."

Whatever she read in his eyes, caused her fingers to tighten on his knee. She removed her hand. "You will remember to be kind, will you not?"

Whose part did she take in this game? He had no clue as to her ultimate goal. And so, he smiled with a hint of the savagery he felt. "Perhaps that depends on one's definition of kindness. Allow me to escort you home to the castle."

SARAH PICKED LISTLESSLY at her breakfast the following morning.

When she had come downstairs, the table in the hall had already been full of flowers and cards, acknowledging her success the previous evening. She had not yet looked at them.

This should have been a joyous day of celebration, when she finally put the past behind her and made plans to go home to her parents. To show them what she had become without them.

Ha. It seemed she was still a lost little girl.

But certainly, she needed to get away from Whitmore, from Arcadi, and, most especially, from any sight of the duke. Lady Whitmore would surely convey them to Durham, from where they could easily hire a chaise to Milforth Park, her father's main seat in Berkshire.

She wished to give no appearance of rushing, but if she spoke to Lady Whitmore today, perhaps two days to pack up the cottage...

She sat back, pushing her still full plate away from her. *I shall miss you, little cottage.*

In fact, what the devil would she do at Milforth Park? Go to parties? Display all her accomplishments like the plumage of a bird looking for a mate?

I'm not. I don't want a mate.

Vaguely, she was aware of the maid answering a knock on the front door, of Hammy's voice in the tiny hall, but she could summon no interest. Perhaps she should walk up to the castle now.

The dining room door opened, and Hammy came in looking flustered. "He's here, with gifts for you."

Sarah blinked. "Gifts? Who is here?"

"The duke!"

Blood sang in her ears. She gripped the edge of her seat. "I cannot accept his gifts. Tell him I have gone out or something. What does he want?"

At the last, Hammy smiled. "There is only one way to find out! Make up your mind, Sarah. Ask him, or send him away. But do not be so cowardly as to request me to do it for you."

Sarah colored, accepting the reproof as fair. Trying to squash the panic, she rose and hastily smoothed her hair—an act that was not lost on the observant Hammy.

"Is he in the parlor?" she asked with a fair imitation of carelessness.

Hammy nodded, and Sarah left the room, trying to slow her breathing and the galloping of her heart. His visit was entirely unexpected. But he could only have come to quarrel, to accuse.

The parlor door was open. She could see the duke standing, gazing out of the window, his hands behind his back. On the table beside him stood a box wrapped in a yellow ribbon and an elegant posy of wild flowers. She doubted they were his. She drew a deep breath, ready to endure his anger.

He turned to face her and smiled. "Good morning. How do you contrive to look more beautiful each time I see you?"

This amiable, light-hearted flirting took her by complete surprise. Was it some cruel joke?

"I d-don't," she stammered.

"Then it must be nature." He bowed and picked the flowers up from the table. "I brought you these, though I wasn't quite sure of the etiquette in the circumstances."

She lifted her chin. "Because we quarrelled?"

His eyebrow flew up. "Did we? I meant the circumstances of you being a lady of birth, rather than a lady of the stage."

Since he still held them out to her, she took them automatically. "Thank you." She laid them down again on the same table. "I imagine you have given many such to ladies of the stage."

"And of birth," he said tranquilly. "Although I can promise I have never given anyone anything as exquisite as *this*." He indicated the beribboned box.

She didn't move. "I cannot accept gifts from Your Grace. It would not be proper."

He considered her. "Can this really be the girl who sat beside me on a tree branch, throwing apples at my carriage?"

"No," she retorted. "We are agreed I have grown up."

"Then indulge me. As a friend of your family, I surely have a right to make you a birthday gift."

She hesitated, even glanced around for Hammy who, most improperly, had not accompanied her into the room.

Then she untied the ribbon and removed the lid from the box. Slowly, she lifted out the alabaster sculpture within. It was the mischievous child.

She raised her gaze to his and found his eyes

gleaming with laughter. It was an effort not to answer with a spontaneous smile of her own.

"I thought you would like it," he said.

"I do. And you are most kind."

"I am, for I admit I would like it as my own. But it should be yours. I daresay you even know the sculptor."

"I do," she managed.

"He is very talented."

"Yes, she is."

He let out a crack of laughter that almost undid her.

Abruptly, she turned, pacing away from him. "Why do you make me gifts? Are you not disgusted with me?"

For a moment, he was silent. She even wondered if he had gone. And then he spoke so close behind her that she jumped. "How could I be disgusted by a kiss like that?"

Her cheeks burned, but she forced herself to turn and face him. "If not by the kiss, then by the motive behind it. I led you on."

"To win a game, I know. To make me propose, so that you could reject me."

It made her ashamed to hear, but she held his gaze bravely. "Exactly."

He smiled. "Then play on, my dear Sarah, for you have not yet won."

Her eyes widened with incomprehension.

He leaned closer, so close she could smell his

soap, the faint scent of coffee on his breath. "I did not ask you to marry me."

"You kissed me!" she said indignantly.

His lips quirked. "You cannot be so naïve as to believe a kiss means marriage. Besides, you are underage. In theory, I should first ask your father's permission to pay my addresses to you."

"Why don't you ask him if you may kiss me?" she retorted. "That is a conversation I *would* like to hear!"

He grinned. "I'll bet you would. But marriage is, by nature, a public business. Kissing is a much more private affair."

She glared at him, and tried to snatch back her hand when he took it in his. His fingers loosened at once, and perversely, she chose to leave it there.

"Come, Sarah," he said softly. "Admit the game has been fun, and let us finish it with a wager."

"A wager?" she repeated, thrown. "For what?"

"For the sculpture." He jerked his head toward the table. "You may keep it and win all honors if I ask you to marry me before I leave Whitmore. But if you kiss me before then, you must give me back the statue."

Butterflies soared in her stomach, dissipating the nervous knot that had gathered there. "Why?" she asked suspiciously.

He smiled. "Fun, of course." He raised her hand to his lips and kissed her fingers.

The touch of his mouth burned, arousing. She struggled for something witty to say and found nothing.

He released her. "Now, I must go. James has found some people to help us dig."

"Dig?" she repeated. She thought she must be going mad.

"For Viking treasure. Feel free to come and see." With that, he stepped back and bowed, then strode jauntily away, letting himself out of the cottage. She even heard him whistling as he strode off up the street.

CHAPTER SIX

"YOU ARE RATHER satisfied this morning, considering what befell you last night, Your Grace," Lady Whitmore said as Leonard placed his breakfast plate, piled high with scrambled eggs, sausage, and bacon, on the table. "Are you back in the game?"

The duke glanced about the comfortable room, finding only two footmen present, then gazed at her, unafraid to speak frankly. "I have left that decision to your lovely guest."

"You went to see her this morning?"

"I did."

"And how would you describe her state of mind?" Lady Whitmore dipped her toast into her cup of coffee, then nibbled on the end of the bread.

"Conflicted."

Lady Whitmore smiled. "I am happy to hear it."

"You wish Miss Sarah to be unsettled?"

"It gives me hope, Your Grace, that all the time she has spent here has not been wasted. If she appears conflicted, it means her conscience is bothering her. Revenge is a heavy burden to carry around for one so young. Her first instinct is to protect herself against you, and she did what she thought best at the height of emotions. But after having a night to contemplate her actions, she has shown that she owns a woman's heart."

"That remains to be seen," he jested.

Lady Whitmore tsked at him.

"Forgive me," he said. "I am overly excited about the possibilities of what we will find once we start excavating today."

"Ah, you are a true scientist. Something I admire."

"Have you considered our earlier discussion? Is there a parcel of land or cottage you would consider selling me, Lady Whitmore? Though an estate or a small farm appeals to me, I wish to stay as close to the digging site as I can."

She studied his face silently, drinking her coffee and finishing her second piece of toast before she spoke again. "Do you know how I came to inherit Whitmore, Your Grace?"

"I am curious, for it is a substantial property for a woman to own."

"Yes, fifteen thousand acres in total, and the castle." She leaned forward, fire in her eyes. "My father sired no sons. But he loved his daughters fiercely. As the eldest, Whitmore, unentailed of course, was always meant for me. Even when I married, my father made sure this property could never be taken away from me."

"Only a shrewd man with significant wealth could achieve such a legal feat."

"Yes. There are loopholes in the law that provide women with property rights if her family is determined and well-connected."

"And your sisters?"

"I have three surviving sisters."

"Were they as fortunate as you?"

"Oh, yes. Father gifted them with prosperous estates, too. My family has strong ties with the Norse, Your Grace. Northern England is filled with our history and kin." She smiled.

"Do you have children of your own?"

The question went unanswered, for his hostess seemed haunted by something as she stared out the window that provided a view of the sea.

"Lady Whitmore?"

"A son," she spoke up unexpectedly.

"He must be very proud of the work you do here."

"Unfortunately, he has never met me. We were separated when he was only three, and I have not seen or communicated with him since then." She gazed into his eyes, the same way she had stared out across the sea.

The story pierced his heart, for what son would not want to be with her? "I am sorry for your loss."

Leonard understood the suffering that went along with being deprived of a beloved parent. His mother had died not long after giving birth to him. As for his father, he had kept a mistress but had never expressed an interest in marrying again. They were not particularly close, but when together, they did have a mutual respect for one another. When the old duke died, it had hurt him deeply.

In defense of the woman he had grown to admire on his short visit, he said, "Is there anything I can do to assist you in reuniting with your son?"

Her eyes grew wide. "You would do that for me?"

"Madam," he said resolutely, "I am your servant."

Tears filled her eyes, and she dabbed at them with her linen napkin. "Excuse me, Your Grace, I am not usually this sentimental." She sniffed delicately and cleared her throat, then took a deep, restorative breath. "I believe you asked if I was willing to part with a piece of my land?"

"Yes, but that can wait, Lady Whitmore."

"I am only too happy to sell you the parcel where you will be digging for treasure. There is a cottage included with the ten acres, Your Grace."

He considered it. Indeed, it would please him to have a stake in Whitmore, not only for the history, but for the women he felt obligated to protect now. Yes, even Sarah seemed to need his help—she just didn't know it yet.

"I will have my solicitor take the necessary steps, Lady Whitmore."

"You may call me Julia in this informal setting, Your Grace."

"Julia?" he repeated.

"Yes."

The duke did not believe in coincidence, however, he did believe in fate, as cruel as she could be at times. "Are you aware, Lady Whitmore, Julia was my mother's name?"

WEARING HER FAVORITE walking dress, bonnet, and leather boots, Sarah could no longer resist the temptation to see what the duke meant exactly by digging. She had strolled along this beach hundreds of times alone, day and night. One of the greatest luxuries afforded the women staying on Lady Whitmore's estate was the freedom to safely explore without a chaperone—in London, it would never be permitted!

She knew the general area where the duke might be, and as she grew closer, she could hear men talking, perhaps metal striking stone. She decided to risk walking up one of the lesser hills so she could get a better view of the activities, and found a most fascinating scene before her. A dozen men were busily digging and pounding wooden stakes into the ground. From her vantage point, she could see the square-shape of where they worked, much like a chess board.

It did not take long for Leonard's familiar voice to sound from behind her. "You decided to accept my invitation, then?"

She turned to find him dressed in dirt-covered pantaloons, a construction worker's long-sleeved shirt, and scuffed boots. He had a kerchief tied about his neck, the first four buttons of his shirt undone, revealing hair on his chest. He mopped his forehead with the back of his hand.

"The conditions are not pleasant for a lady," he said.

"I am not afraid of dirt and sweat, Your Grace," she said. "Surely you know that by now."

"Yes, but first impressions and all."

She laughed at his audacity. "Are you comparing this to the first time we met?"

"Well, in fairness, I have seen you at your worst. So, I am happy to return the favor."

"I would not consider this your worst, but more like your natural environment."

He snorted. "As a pig in mud?"

"I never implied that, did I?"

They both chuckled.

"I am intrigued by what you are doing here. History was my favorite subject. Ask my former governess, she had to fight to get my nose out of the history books."

"Do you wish me to explain what you are looking at below?"

"Of course."

"My men are following a grid method of excavation."

"Yes, it reminds me of a chess board."

"Quite right," he said. "There are a number of test pits, perhaps three-by-three yards each, and we preserve the integrity of each square with balks that are half a yard wide. It protects the different layers of soil which can tell us so much. And see..." He gestured below. "The wooden stakes are placed around each pit, and then we tie rope between the stakes to section off the squares."

"Fascinating."

"Would you care to take a tour?"

She nodded and allowed him to take her hand and guide her down the hill and up the shoreline until they reached the area where the men were working.

Lifting her chin and closing her eyes, she breathed in salt air, loving the heat of the sun on her face. "It is beautiful here."

"Yes," he said. "And you make it more so."

She opened her eyes and gazed at him. "You think me beautiful?"

"I think you are a goddess, Sarah."

He bowed slightly, and she fought the urges to run away or kiss him. "Are you flirting with me, Your Grace?"

"I am making my good opinion known."

The turbulence inside her slowed down a bit. Last night, the storm had peaked, and she had gotten little sleep. She had acted abhorrently and owed him an apology. Coming here was her way of offering him an olive branch.

"What do you hope to find here?"

"Artifacts, of course."

She was vaguely aware of his lingering stare at her back as she watched a man lift a shovel full of soil and dump it into a metal sieve. The man holding the sieve walked a short distance and slowly emptied the sieve by shaking it back and forth. A pile of soil had already started to accumulate.

"How long have you been here?"

"Six hours."

"I'm impressed. You seem to be making quick progress."

The two-man team continued their routine, and by the tenth exchange, the one holding the sieve called out, "Found something, Your Grace!"

Sarah followed the duke and reacted as excitedly as he did to the ancient looking drinking vessel the worker held up.

"It's covered in filth, Your Grace, but with careful cleaning, I believe this may be a valuable piece."

Leonard pulled what resembled a small painting brush from his pocket, cradled the vessel in his other hand, and with cautious strokes, began to wipe some of the layers of dirt away.

"Yes," he said, his face lighting up. "Come here, Sarah."

She approached, eager to see what he was looking at.

"Do you recognize what these are?"

Crudely carved into the pottery, there were about sixteen symbols in all. "No."

"Runes," he offered. "The equivalent of the alphabet to the Norse."

"Really?" She studied the blueish-brown piece. "Will you be able to decipher its meaning once it is clean?"

"Perhaps," he said, obviously elated. "There is still much to learn of our Viking conquerors. They did not have a written language, and their history was passed down through stories. Some monuments exist with runic messages on them in Scandinavia."

"You have been there?"

"Three times."

How she envied his freedom, his worldliness.

She wanted to visit the most exotic places. Furthermore, she hadn't known the duke had such a deep passion for anything. It added layers to his otherwise rigid character, making him more appealing to her adventurous spirit. Seeing him this way, dressed as a commoner, hands dirty, filled with such zeal, and the sunshine on his handsome face, she could fall in love with him all over again. Yes... That day in the tree had done her in—she had loved him instantly. Even her brothers had never climbed a tree with her! The fact that a duke had taken the time to join her in her favorite tree had meant something to her.

"What is it, Miss Sarah?"

"Nothing at all," she lied, forcing a smile on her face. "I am thrilled for you, Your Grace. But I am afraid I have overstayed my welcome. I am expected for tea with Lady Whitmore."

"May I escort you to the castle?"

"No," she said too sharply. "I mean, thank you, but I rather enjoy the solitude of my daily walks."

As she wandered away, she realized that was the second time in two days that she had left the Duke of Vexen standing alone and wanting more time with her.

CHAPTER SEVEN

TIRED BUT DELIGHTED with the fruits of his first day's dig, Leonard scrubbed himself clean and changed into evening clothes. He had meant to instruct James to write to his solicitor about the purchase of the cottage and land offered by Lady Whitmore, but his secretary was having dinner with a harpist this evening. Much to Leonard's amusement and secret delight, for he thought James too staid for a young man.

Accordingly, since there was still half an hour or so before dinner, he repaired to Lady Whitmore's library to write his own letter.

The library was empty but finding a quantity of headed notepaper on one of the desks, he sat down and drew a sheet toward him. As he dipped his pen in the ink stand, he read the printed address at the top of the paper: Whitmore Castle, Whitmore, Northumberland. Nowhere mentioned her name or title. Perhaps the paper was also used by the "villagers."

Still, it was not a great deal to give his solicitor who would, presumably discuss matters with her ladyship's man of business. On impulse, he replaced the pen and rose to find out what he could about the estate and its owner.

Discovering bound volumes of Debrett's, he looked up Lady Whitmore—and did not find her. In fact, he could find no peers or even baronets with this name, which made him scratch his head. However, he rarely gave in to problems and began to search elsewhere for information on Whitmore Castle, and this time found much that he meant to pursue at his leisure. In the meantime, he was searching for current ownership.

In the previous century, he learned from a musty tome, Whitmore had been part of the considerable estate owned by Viscount Fordenham. Once more he picked up Debrett's and easily discovered the last viscount, who had indeed died with no male issue. The title had died out. But he had left three daughters: Julia, Marian, and Georgiana.

Which made perfect sense, except that Julia now called herself Lady Whitmore, a title which did not appear to exist. He supposed it was a sort of a courtesy title, such as they used in Scotland, where a landowner might be known by the name of his estate and his wife as Lady of that estate.

Lady Whitmore could have adopted such a practice. After all, she was clearly the great lady of the area.

But she had been married. She had a son. Would she not use their names?

That, perhaps, depended on the reason for her estrangement. It seemed to Leonard that she was as incognito as any of her guests.

But he had run out of time. He stood and made his way to the drawing room to join his hostess.

As her guest, he could hardly show unseemly curiosity. He did, however mention it obliquely by referring to his difficulty in directing his solicitor.

"Oh, it will be simpler if my man contacts yours," she said easily. "How goes your excavation? Have you discovered anything more interesting than pebbles? I do hope you haven't dug up any bones!"

At once, he was distracted into telling her about the cup with the runes, and from there to his encounter with Sarah. The little mystery got lost in the back of his mind for later. And, in fact, he only thought about it again the following morning when two visitors strolled down the hill to his excavation.

At the time, he was crouched over one pit, in deep discussion with James and one of the laborers.

"Hello! Your Grace!" called a familiar voice.

Leonard looked up, shading his eyes against the morning sun, and recognized Trenton and, less welcome, Maria Loxley. He stood, edging around his pits to join them.

He bowed to Maria and offered his hand to Trenton. "What a pleasant surprise. I didn't know you were still in Whitmore."

"Well, we couldn't resist staying another night or two when we heard what you were up to," Trenton said with a grin. "Er, what are you up to?"

"Treasure hunting," Leonard replied. "What are you up to?"

"Plotting," Maria said with a tinkling laugh. "We thought we would hold a little supper dance at the inn. There is decent company in the village—to say nothing of excellent musicians and cooks. Would you come?"

"Of course, if you have Lady Whitmore's permission," Leonard replied, spying an opportunity to dance with Sarah. If only Maria kept her claws to herself.

"Do we need her permission?" Maria wondered. "Certainly, we were on our way to invite her. Oh, look, isn't that her little protégée?"

Leonard quickly followed her gaze and saw Sarah walking across the top of the hill in the direction of the castle. She waved, and Leonard lifted his hand in response.

Trenton swept off his hat and bowed. "What luck!"

"Come, let's hurry and catch up with her," Maria urged, setting off toward the hill.

"I'll walk up with you," Leonard said, reluctantly picking his coat up from the ground and struggling into it. He did not trust Maria's apparent friendship with Sarah.

However, Maria hurried ahead without help, calling to Sarah to wait. Trenton seemed delighted when Sarah obeyed.

Leonard was unreasonably irritated. He wished he wasn't dressed like a grubby laborer while Trenton looked, as always, the perfectly groomed gentleman.

Since Maria linked arms with Sarah, there was nothing for it but to fall behind them. But at least it gave Leonard the chance to question his friend, to look somewhere other than Sarah's enticing, slender body moving so gracefully inside her flimsy gown and spencer.

"Tell me, Trenton, you've been here before, have you not? For Whitmore events?"

"A few now, yes."

"How is that? Do you know her ladyship well?"

"Actually, no—I've only ever met her here. But she's an old friend of my mother's. And of Lady Billows, who first pressed me into escort duty a couple of years ago. Why?"

"Oh, no reason, really. Just trying to work out who she is. I believe the estate is hers, not her husband's."

"Probably."

"Who was her husband?" Leonard asked bluntly.

Trenton frowned with the effort of memory. "Not sure I ever heard. If I did, I've forgotten. Ask my mother next time you see her! Mind you, I've a feeling there might have been some ancient scandal or other. Which probably explains why no one mentions the husband."

"Is he dead?"

Trenton scratched his head. "No idea," he said at last. "Again—ask my mother!"

SARAH HAD TAKEN this path to the castle with the intention of visiting the duke en route. She felt quite disappointed to see he already had visitors, one of whom was the woman who had seemed to warn her off on the night of the exhibition. Even without the uncomfortable twist of jealousy, Sarah would have been in no hurry to renew the acquaintance, so she was not best pleased to be hailed and entreated to wait.

However, there was little she could do without rudeness except wait for the others to catch up. At least she might have opportunity to talk to the duke who had joined them. But it was Lady Loxley who thrust her arm through Sarah's, ignoring the men and chattering instead about a party she wished to hold at the inn.

"Do say you will come," Lady Loxley whispered conspiratorially. "Just between us, my friend Lord Trenton is completely smitten with you."

"I'm sure you are wrong, my lady," Sarah said repressively. Gone were the days when such a revelation could make her blush. Besides, it seemed she cared little for Trenton's opinion, amiable as he was. Her every waking—and sleeping!—thought tended to revolve around the infuriating duke.

As soon as she civilly could, she drew free of Lady Loxley's clinging arm—a freedom she immediately regretted, as the lady seized Vexen's arm instead, scolding him for his grime in a laughing and familiar way.

Sarah took Lord Trenton's proffered arm with a quick smile and concentrated on answering his friendly conversation. However, she was undeniably relieved when they came to the castle and were shown through to the back of the house and outside into a pleasant walled garden where Lady Whitmore sat before an easel.

"Ah, visitors!" Lady Whitmore exclaimed, rising to her feet. "How delightful! Now I may give up this quite unsuccessful watercolor without feeling guilty in the least. Saunders, send out some tea if you would, and perhaps a little luncheon. Come, sit here in the shade…"

They sat around a table, which had been placed with some chairs under a willow tree, and Lady Loxley immediately launched into her supper dance idea. "What do you think?" she asked their hostess.

"I think it sounds charming."

"Then we may count on your attendance? Even with so little notice?"

"Of course," Lady Whitmore replied graciously. "I gather all here will be present?"

"If His Grace promises to clean his fingernails," Lady Loxley teased.

"They shall be scrubbed and cut, and my hands rendered as soft as your own," the duke said wryly.

"Then I might condescend to dance with you," Lady Loxley said, smiling at him.

He held her gaze. "I might condescend to ask you. Lady Whitmore, your cook has a way with scones. They are the most delicious I've ever eaten."

Sarah held her own during the ensuing conversation. Although she never thrust herself forward, she liked to think she made a few light, witty responses and added several sensible opinions when called upon. But Lady Loxley jangled her nerves, and she was glad when the party broke up.

"Come, you may walk with us back to your burial site," Lady Loxley said indulgently.

"Sadly, I must forgo that delight," the duke replied. "I have matters to attend to here first."

Sarah, suddenly appalled at the prospect of having to walk back to the village with Lady Loxley and Trenton, searched wildly for an excuse to stay a while longer. "Did you find the music we spoke of, Lady Whitmore?"

"Oh, drat, no, I forgot to look," her hostess replied. "Never mind. Come in and rummage now."

Relieved, Sarah curtsied to the rest of the company and followed Lady Whitmore into the castle. From the corner of her eye, she caught the duke's crooked smile and knew he had seen through her excuse. She couldn't help wondering if he, too, was avoiding Lady Loxley, or even—intoxicating thought—making an excuse to spend time with her.

"Here is where I keep my music," Lady Whitmore said, indicating the chest beside the pianoforte. "If indeed you care."

"Forgive me, I didn't mean to be rude to you or your guests. I hope they are not great friends of yours."

Lady Whitmore shrugged elegantly. "Trenton's mother is one of my oldest friends, and I am fond of the boy for her sake. Maria Loxley's husband was one of our most generous patrons. I still invite her, though this is the first time she has actually come. I suspect Vexen is the attraction."

Sarah opened her mouth to ask about any relationship, then swiftly closed it again. She could not be so unseemly.

Lady Whitmore smiled with a little too much understanding and flitted away, leaving Sarah to look through the music—which turned out to be quite a treasure trove. Among other exciting finds, she discovered an older variation of a Scottish song she loved and was singing it softy to herself when she became aware of being observed.

She broke off, lifting her gaze from the music to the French doors where the Duke of Vexen leaned one broad shoulder, watching her intently.

"Don't stop," he said. "It's beautiful."

"It is," she agreed with enthusiasm. "I have never come across this version before—it is much deeper and somehow even more sad."

He smiled, easing his shoulder off the wall and walking into the room. "Your voice has something to do with it, too. You are modest for a pupil of Signor Arcadi."

"Oh, don't," Sarah said with a shudder. "He has left Whitmore and refuses to come back until I am gone."

"Good."

Sarah's eyes fell. She tucked the bound music under her arm, and closed the chest. "I must go. Hammy is expecting me."

"May I walk with you as far as my site? Or is solitude still more alluring?"

She flushed. "I shall be glad of the company."

He smiled and offered her his arm.

"Do you have plans to leave Whitmore?" he asked as they walked across the outer courtyard.

"Soon," she replied. Her smile twisted. "Lady Billows said my parents miss me. Do you think that is true?"

"Why should you doubt it?"

"Well, they barely noticed me when I was with them. Unless I misbehaved."

"Sometimes we don't appreciate what we have until it is too late. Don't leave it too long to go to them, for I think *you* miss *them*. Speaking as someone who knows the loss of parents, I would do anything to spend an hour with mine."

"Truly?" She regarded him curiously. For the most part, he was so self-possessed, so independent that she had never imagined him feeling the vulnerability of loss. "You were very little, you said, when your mother died. Do you remember her?"

"I remember an impression, a soft voice, a comforting scent. But I doubt the features of her face bore any resemblance to my memory."

She caught a glimpse of a child's baffled grief,

a loneliness worse than any she had known. "And your father?" she asked gently.

"I remember him better. But he was a distant figure. I never felt he liked me very much and wished he did. But I was too young, too proud to worm my way into reluctant affections. And then he died, and it was too late." He made a dismissive gesture with his hand, as though banishing regret and sadness, "Which is why I think you should go home, why Lady Whitmore—" He broke off.

"Lady Whitmore?" she repeated in surprise.

He hesitated. Then, "Apparently she has a son from whom she is estranged. But she will not let me help or even tell me who he is. I can find no likely candidates in Debrett's. I daresay she would consider it prying in any case. But if you get the chance, you might urge her in the direction of reunion."

Sarah smiled. "Your Grace is unexpectedly kind."

"Your Grace," he repeated with derision. "I think at least in private you might call me by name."

"Leonard," she remembered.

"Some of my older friends call me Leo."

"And here is where I must leave you, Leo." They had walked as far as the track down the hill to his site and she stopped, offering her hand.

He smiled as though his name on her lips

pleased him. He took her hand in his warm clasp and bowed over it. "No complaints about grimy fingernails?"

She smiled back. "Considering how we met, I would be a pot calling the kettle black."

"Then I will see you at the inn tomorrow evening. I hope you'll save a waltz for me."

She only laughed and set off again toward the village. She wondered if they were still playing, or if the flirting was real.

CHAPTER EIGHT

ONCE AGAIN, THE duke found himself watching with amazement as Sarah walked away—her level of grace and comportment, something he deeply admired. As for himself... He would not deny himself the chance to kiss her again. The path she took home had several areas with thick trees where no one would see them.

"Sarah," he called as he strode after her.

Perhaps she didn't hear him, or maybe she didn't wish to, but kept walking, staring up at the sky, then straight ahead.

Though he appreciated the chase as much as any other man did, Leonard was not one to do so out in the open. He glanced to his left and right, finding no one on the road. Then, "Sarah."

She stopped but did not turn around.

"It seems you are forgetting something, sweeting," he said.

"Oh?" This time she did pivot and offered

him a naughty smile. "And what would that be, Your Grace?"

"That first kiss was a boon."

She appeared completely unaware of what he referred to. "What kiss?"

Now only a foot away from her, he looked into her eyes. "Do you require a reminder?"

"Out here? Even you would not be so bold!"

"I am many things, Sarah."

She crossed her arms over her chest, her cheeks coloring. "It must not have been memorable, for any thought of it is gone."

He snorted, appreciative of her resilience and ability to give out as good as she got. "There's no one to impress here, Sarah. Just you and I—two people with history. I know for certain you remember that."

"I forget things as a manner of protecting myself."

"From whom?"

"Many people."

"If this is about your parents again..." Her lack of self-worth where her parents were concerned pulled at his heartstrings.

She shook her head.

"If not your parents, who? Has Arcadi threatened you? Is there another man?"

"Nothing so dramatic. I just feel no matter what I do..." Her hands clenched and she looked away. "Why should I discuss such intimate things with you? You remain the biggest reason why I am here."

"Sarah." He wondered what had changed in the few steps she had taken after their walk together. But women were accorded the luxury of changing their minds. Like a northward wind suddenly becoming a westward breeze. One simply did not question the reasons why. "How may I help ease your suffering?"

Before she could answer, he took her hand and ushered her into the trees, hoping for more privacy. "If it provides some reassurance, Sarah, I am here now. Your charms are many and irresistible. The wild girl in that tree is long behind you, though I'd like to think part of her still remains."

Her eyelashes fluttered attractively as she stared up at him. "And what part of her did you like most?"

"Her spirit."

She swallowed hard, her gaze raking over him. He found her reaction mysterious, but leaned forward and placed a chaste kiss on her lips. If he did not test the waters, he would never get a true idea of how she felt. When she did not object to the light show of affection, he wrapped his arms about her and pulled her into a solid embrace, her cheek resting on his chest.

His body, ever susceptible to hers, responded favorably to the contact, his pantaloons tighter and suddenly uncomfortable. He shifted on his feet, trying to find relief, but it didn't work.

"What do you want from me?" she asked, once again surprising him.

He held her at arm's length and grinned at her. "I would think that is rather obvious. A real kiss."

"You seem to give out kisses quite freely, Your Grace."

He chuckled, then claimed what he had pursued her for. He slanted his mouth over hers, coaxing her lips apart with his skilled tongue, seeking her warmth and acceptance—wanting to taste her over and over again. She sighed, her hand slipping up his shoulder and to his nape, cupping the back of his neck. Sarah leaned into him, her firm breasts pushing against his chest, her slim body his to hold and feel.

Yes. Just as her personality, Sarah's body possessed ample contradictions—slight yet curved in all the right places, soft yet firm from her daily walks, strong yet weak, for her legs trembled and he had to prop her up. He smiled against her mouth, appreciating everything she had to offer.

"Why are you smiling?" she whispered. "Are my kisses lacking in skill?"

"If you only knew…" He buried his fingers in her hair, pins coming loose, and her hat fell to the ground. He couldn't stop, and pulled her tresses down, thick, black curls cascaded down her back. It smelled of lavender and sunshine. "You are beautiful."

"If we are caught together like this…"

"*If* is an important word, Lady Sarah. For *if* we are not…" He tasted her again and again, the need mutual, the desire to stop banished. His hands moved lower, tracing the lines of her bottom, then gently caressing and holding. He groaned, awakened, wanting more. But Leonard knew he should stop, had to, in fact. He was no beast but found himself acting as one. She deserved better. He wanted to offer her the world but couldn't until he was sure this was not a game of revenge.

He pulled back and took in the lovely sight of her, black hair hopelessly tangled from his fingers and the cooling breeze, her lips swollen from his hard kisses, her eyes wide with wonder, as were his, for he had never been this reckless.

"I am a mess," she observed, trying to twist her hair into a loose bun. "I do not think I could explain away my appearance, even to Lady Whitmore."

He thought for a moment, he must protect her. "There is a lake several yards from here."

"Yes?"

"Hidden on this side by the woods."

"I am familiar with the place," she said.

"Forgive me." He scooped her into his arms

and rushed through the trees, ignoring her complaints to be put down. Once they reached the lake, he looked down at her, smiled, then tossed her into the water.

She landed with a splash, then surged up, waving her arms angrily, cursing him.

"Hold on, sweeting," he called, then jumped in after her.

"You rogue!" She slapped his chest and shoulder as he attempted to pull her into his arms. "I am not an experienced swimmer," she complained. "I could drown."

"Sarah," he said, standing up, the water reaching his thighs. "If you stand up…"

"Oh!" She did as instructed, glaring at him. "My gown is ruined."

"Better than a ruined reputation," he growled, picking her up just as a couple started to come their way. "I am sorry I pointed out the swan," Leonard said. "I never thought you would slip in the mud, Miss Sarah. Thank God I was here to rescue you!"

"Leo," she muttered through clenched teeth so only he could hear, "if ever I am alone with you again…"

"Yes, sweeting, I know. You will kill me for sure. But at this moment, if you could play the shaken debutante."

She wilted in his arms suddenly and uttered a feminine moan.

"Leonard, Your Grace!" Maria Loxley raised

her hand and came running. "What has happened to Miss Sarah?"

Could he never rid himself of the woman? But her usefulness at this moment could not be denied.

"I'm afraid our lovely siren has taken a fall into the lake."

"We had better get her to the castle," Trenton said, appearing deeply concerned.

"You are soaked to the bone, too, Your Grace. Perhaps Lord Trenton should relieve you of your burden, and I can help you get back to the castle so you don't catch a cold."

Leonard rolled his eyes. "Why don't we all go together?" He did not wait for a reply, but strode toward the castle, holding in his need to release the laughter building up inside of him. He had won this battle with Sarah, though not the war. He could not remember a more enjoyable afternoon than this, nor a more pleasing sight than the wet material of Sarah's gown, translucent and clinging to her breasts, revealing more of her than he should ever see at this point in their relationship.

But, God in heaven, she was beautiful. And to have her in his arms like this—he gave her rear a subtle squeeze, and she nearly jumped out of his arms.

Finding the tender skin of his underarm, she pinched him so hard, he yelped.

"Your Grace?" Maria came to his side. "Are

you hurt? Is she too heavy for you to carry further?"

Sarah, unable to stay silent any longer, said, "Please put me down, Your Grace. I can walk now."

IT SHOULDN'T HAVE been funny, but somehow, despite being so cold and wet, the duke's silent laughter seemed to be infectious. She could feel his vibrating chest and shoulders through her own shivering and without the energy for anger, she had a dangerous urge to giggle. After all, "falling" in the lake was an ingenious explanation for her tousled appearance.

At least when he finally set her on her feet, she did not have to fight her body's wayward reactions to his touch. On the other hand, she missed his warmth. And her clothing clung to her like a second skin, which was horribly embarrassing.

She could not look at Leo for fear of laughing, or at any of them for fear of blushing. So she walked faster, saying breathlessly, "You must think me very clumsy for losing my footing like that, but truly I did not expect His Grace to be quite so enthusiastic about a swan!"

"Alas," the duke mourned, "I believe it was

your own enthusiasm that caused you to turn so quickly and slip."

"And he clearly jumped in to rescue you," Lady Loxley pointed out.

"Waded in," Sarah corrected, risking a glance at Leonard, who looked hastily away, biting his lip.

"I acknowledge it was all my fault," he said shakily, and Sarah let out a snort of laughter that she hoped might be mistaken for anger.

Lady Whitmore took the return of her guests—two of them soaked to the skin—quite in her stride, merely summoning servants to aid the afflicted.

Only as Sarah hurried upstairs in the wake of a maid did their hostess interrupt the flow of Lord Trenton's explanations to demand in dismay, "Sarah? Is my music ruined?"

"Oh, no," Leonard said from several stairs beneath. He held the leather-bound sheets over the bannister to Lord Trenton, who passed them to Lady Whitmore.

Sarah paused, her mouth falling open. Had she dropped the music? When had he picked it up? She had forgotten all about it in the midst of passion and the shock of her cold soak.

Leonard smiled at her tranquilly, and this time she could not hold in the laughter. She actually ran after the maid, hoping her mirth would be misconstrued as feminine hysterics.

CHAPTER NINE

THE FOLLOWING AFTERNOON, Leonard and James left the dig early in order to prepare for the supper party at the inn. James was clearly eager to see his harpist again, and Leonard... Well, it had been an effort to stay away from Sarah today. He hadn't seen her since they had parted soaked to the skin in the castle.

Her warmth, her passion, delighted him, as did the shared if concealed hilarity of their dip in the lake. But she was skittish, unsure, and that haunted him. Could he really be responsible for the uncertainty that lay beneath her outward charm? Had his act of walking away from her two years ago—an act he had considered so honorable at the time—truly affected her so deeply?

Guilt tugged at his heart. She had told him he was the reason she was here, making herself a perfect and accomplished lady to capture his heart. Not to marry him but to reject him.

Revenge, which he had inspired.

He hadn't meant to be cruel. But at the very least he had been thoughtless. And now she did not trust him—or any man.

Deep in thought, he entered the castle by a side door, James at his heels. At once he was aware of someone descending the stairs that led to Lady Whitmore's private apartments, and paused to greet her.

But it was not her ladyship, but his own man of business.

"Jenkins," he said in surprise. "How on earth did you get my letter so quickly?"

Jenkins's eyes had widened with equal astonishment, so that he looked positively alarmed. "Oh, I have not had your letter, sir. I came in response to...er... In short, sir, your hostess is one of my oldest and most honored clients."

Leonard blinked. "Is she, by God? You mean we share a solicitor?" He laughed. "What are the odds?"

Jenkins smiled nervously. "A useful coincidence however. We are agreed you shall rent the property you discussed. I have left papers for you to sign if you find the rent fair, which I think it is."

"I would rather buy it and be done," Leonard said with a frown.

"Unhappily, her...her ladyship is not in a position to sell. Although the property is settled upon her, she needs to keep it intact to be passed on to her son."

"Oh. Well, I would not care to step on her son's toes."

"To be sure, sir, that would look most odd," Jenkins said breathlessly.

Leonard peered at him. "Are you quite well, Jenkins?"

"Indeed, sir. But Your Grace must forgive me. A conveyance to Durham awaits me…"

Still frowning, Leonard watched him dash through the passage to the main hall. "Does it seem to you, James, that everyone has run mad?"

"Present company excepted, my lord Duke."

"Oh, no, not at all," Leonard said ruefully and carried on to his chamber.

AS SHE AND Hammy entered the inn that evening, Sarah's heart beat with excitement. She knew it was foolish, but she was in danger of believing in the duke's warmth toward her. Not his attraction to her. She had deliberately won that from the beginning. And even if she had given him the wrong idea about her morals, she knew from the lust in his eyes—and his body, God help her— that he still desired her. But then he had, presumably, once desired Lady Loxley and probably still did. Sarah refused to be one in a long line of flirts, to call it no worse. And if Leonard had mentioned marriage in his wager proposal, he had not offered it. What if he merely wanted revenge on the chit who had fooled him? If she believed in his courtship, in the warmth of true friendship growing between them... If she kissed him and lost the wager... well then, she lost everything.

Have I not already lost my heart? If she hadn't, would her gaze have flown around the inn's upper hall in immediate search of him?

She saw him at once, tall and immaculately well groomed, talking to Jenny the harpist, a shy young lady who had become a friend of Sarah's. Jenny was also extremely pretty, and Sarah was ashamed to acknowledge she would have been jealous had the other girl's gaze not flickered so frequently to Mr. James, who stood nearby.

"Miss Sarah!" cooed Lady Loxley, offering a slightly limp but perfectly gloved hand. "How lovely to see you here. I was afraid you might have taken some hurt after your terrible experience yesterday."

"Oh, no. The only casualty was my dignity," Sarah assured her.

"And Vexen's," Lady Loxley reminded her gently.

Sarah laughed. "Oh, no. I'm sure His Grace enjoyed the adventure." She passed on to let the last of the guests be greeted.

She and Hammy were making their way toward Lady Whitmore when the trio of musicians in the far corner—all friends of Sarah's—struck up a country dance.

A poet by the name of Lovelace stood in front of her, smiling. "Miss Sarah, will you do me the honor?"

It was a lively dance, guaranteed to banish anxiety and awkwardness, and Sarah thoroughly enjoyed it. If she found time to note—with amusement—that Leonard danced in the other set, partnered by the sculptress of the statue of the mischievous child, well it detracted nothing from the fun of the dance.

From there, she was swept straight into another dance with Lord Trenton and was ridiculously thrilled to see Leonard watching her broodingly from one corner of the room.

"Won't you make me happy by promising me the next dance also?" Lord Trenton asked as they twirled together near the end of the set.

"Oh, not the next one!" she pleaded. "I must sit it out, or I shall expire!"

Lord Trenton laughed good naturedly. "Then at least allow me to fetch you wine? Or lemonade."

"Either would be most welcome." She took his arm as the dance came to a close, and he began to escort her back toward Hammy. Her heart gave a funny little lurch when she saw the gentleman seated beside her old governess. Leonard.

He stood, bowing with his always perfect grace. "I'm very glad to see you recovered," he said gravely.

"Likewise," she replied.

"Allow me to fetch that lemonade," Trenton said. "Miss Hammy, may I bring you anything?"

Sarah never heard Hammy's answer. She was lost in Leonard's compelling gaze, in the memory of what those exquisite lips could do.

He held out his hand. "Dance with me?"

She swallowed. "I just told Lord Trenton I was too tired to dance again."

"It's a waltz," Leonard observed as the opening strains began. "Barely dancing at all."

A breath of laughter shook her.

"Go on," he encouraged. "Trenton may have another dance instead, after all."

Hammy was frowning at her, scandalized that she might turn down a request to dance with a duke. And yet, when she took his hand, it was because she wanted to.

"That's my girl," he said, leading her onto the floor.

"I am not," she pointed out crossly.

"Not *yet*." He turned and took her into his arms. Heat swept through her, and he took her by surprise, beginning to dance before she was ready. She stumbled the first steps, annoyed with herself for being so clumsy and gauche, hardly the way to endear herself to this man.

But he did not appear to notice. His gaze held hers as surely as his arm held her body. She recovered quickly, following his guide, his rhythm. His nearness, the almost-touch of his body, excited her.

He smiled, his thumb stroking against her palm. "I have always wanted to dance with you."

"Yes, I imagine it was your first thought when you saw the urchin hurling apples at your coach."

"*Ah, she throws an accurate fruit,* I said to my-self, *but can she waltz with the grace of a gliding swan?*"

She narrowed her eyes. "Don't mention swans to me, Leonard Vexen."

A breath of laughter escaped him. "I apologize for the lake. But you must admit it was effective. Another few minutes, and our friends would have come upon us alone together, and seen you with your hair wild and tumbled. Exactly like a young lady who has been well and truly kissed."

Her cheeks burned. So did the rest of her, but she refused to drop her gaze. Instead, she titled her chin. "I find it ungentlemanly of you to mention such a subject."

"But not ungentlemanly that I did it?" he asked with interest.

She held his gaze. "No."

A smile flickered across his lips. His thigh brushed against her, shocking and arousing. "Why not?"

"I was complicit. I let you. But you have not won the wager."

"No, you have to kiss me for that," he agreed. Surely he held her too close now? "I am at your disposal."

"I will let you know. Please don't hold your breath in anticipation."

He grinned. "I won't. But I am more than happy to do the kissing for both of us. There is an alcove behind that curtain…"

"I do not make assignations. Certainly not with gentlemen who drop me in lakes."

"But I cannot kiss you in public."

"No," she said triumphantly, "you cannot."

A speculative gleam lit his eyes, weakening her knees with as much desire as alarm.

"You would not dare!" she whispered.

"We have had this conversation before," he pointed out. "But, no. Reluctantly, I have to admit that I would not kiss you here. The alcove now…"

"No."

His eyes laughed beguilingly, and she realized with some awe that he was only flirting with her. Flirting with a rather thrilling edge, it had to be said, but she understood at last that he would do nothing to hurt her. The banter between them was fun, exciting, and curiously comfortable.

She had the impression she was falling deeper and deeper. And she liked it.

EVERY MOMENT HE spent with her was delight, and yet left him longing for more. As the waltz ended—much too soon—he hadn't given up hope of enticing her into that alcove later in the evening. In the meantime, he had the annoyance of seeing her go off on Trenton's arm almost as soon as he had returned her to Miss Hammy.

"Don't look like that, my pet," drawled an amused female voice in his ear. Maria Loxley, of course.

"Like what? And I believe I stopped being your pet some years ago and became a *vile, insensitive idiot* instead."

"Like a dog in the manger," she replied, ignoring the second part of his speech. She took his arm and walked with him toward the supper room. "Don't begrudge poor Trenton his love affair. Or Miss Sarah. He can't marry her, of course, but he will be a kind and generous benefactor."

He frowned down at her. "You have no idea who she is, have you?"

"Why? Do tell."

He shrugged. "The secret is not mine. But trust me, her birth is quite equal to his."

"Oh, well perhaps he will marry her, then" Maria said with a delight that grated on him. "I will allow they look very well together, don't you think?"

No!

"And he is very smitten with her. He doesn't seem to mind her clumsiness."

In the supper room, he managed to lose Maria, eventually, and fell into a conversation about literature with two young men who looked vaguely familiar. One wrote poetry. It was as he returned to the main room that he saw Sarah, free of partners for once, lift a glass from a waiter's tray. She looked vaguely surprised, and Leonard saw that she had picked something up with it. It looked like a folded scrap of paper.

A secret note.

Jealousy clawed at him so hard it felt like rage. How dare someone send her secret messages? Well, she would not read it…

Sitting beside Hammy, she read it, pretending to look in her reticule for something. Her beautiful face looked flushed, excited, rather like when he kissed her.

Trenton?

He turned away, seething, and yet hating himself for it. He refused to make too much of nothing. And so, he danced with James's harpist.

The dance had had no sooner finished than Maria Loxley was again at his side. Only this time, she looked concerned.

"Come with me," she murmured. "There's something I have to show you. Subtly, my dear…"

He almost laughed when he found himself facing the curtain to the alcove he had tried to entice Sara to. And then his heart twisted, for it came to him Maria meant to show him Trenton and Sarah together. Damn the woman, it would be just like her.

He reached up and pulled back the curtain. Quick as lightning, Maria slipped through and he followed, his stomach hollow.

The alcove was empty.

With relief turning hastily to irritation, he demanded, "What the devil are you up to? What do you have to show me here?"

"This," she said, winding her arms around his neck and pressing herself to him as she kissed him.

Once, he had found Maria's charms irresistible. But there had been little behind her beauty to appeal to him. Any feeling for her had long since vanished. In his heart and his thoughts was only Sarah.

He took hold of her wrists, forcing her away from him. "Our time is past," he said. "What do you want, Maria?"

"Marriage. You know I would make a perfect duchess."

"I know—" He broke off, warned by some glint in her eyes that looked almost like triumph. He jerked his head around, dropping her hands. The curtain swished, as though someone had brushed against it. "I know you and I would not suit. You must find another duke. Find a prince, a king—I wish you well. But you and I, Maria? No."

Only when he had walked out and the curtain fell back behind him did it enter his head that she had not looked unhappy. Perhaps in her heart, she knew their affair could never be rekindled.

Drawing a breath as though clearing the air, he looked around, as he always seemed to, for Sarah. And found her waltzing with Trenton, her face still flushed, her eyes sparkling and brilliant as she laughed up at him.

Just as she had with Leonard.

CHAPTER TEN

W HAT HAD THAT awful saying been she heard her father say so often to her mother… *What's sauce for the goose is sauce for the gander?* Well, if the duke wished to have an affair with another woman while he was carrying on with her… She was no goose, but a woman with passions of her own, with newly awakened hopes of happiness. How dare he treat her with such contempt?

Looking at Lord Trenton more closely, she realized what a handsome man he truly was. Surely, he would never play with her heart, not as Leonard just had—holding and kissing Lady—not much of a lady—Loxley in the very alcove the duke had tried to pull her into.

Were all men so lascivious or just her duke?

"What is it, Miss Sarah?" Lord Trenton asked as he turned her about on the dance floor.

"Nothing," she lied. "Perhaps I am just overheated and tired after my swim today."

He nodded in understanding and immediately escorted her off the dance floor and over to Hammy. He bowed over Sarah's hand. "If you find yourself feeling better, I will be close." He took his leave.

"What are you up to?" Hammy asked as Sarah sat down next to her.

"What you would consider no good," she answered rather tight-lipped as she searched the crowd for the duke.

"You do know," Hammy started, "that you could put an end to his suffering and yours if you'd just admit…"

"That he destroyed my life the day he rejected me?"

"Well, yes, if you wish to put it that simply."

"Look at him," she breathed. "There is nothing simple about that man."

"Nor you."

Sarah thought about that as darker feelings swirled inside her—the emotions that often overtook her when her confidence slipped. In all actuality, she knew she possessed the feminine charms to bring someone like Lord Trenton to his knees. Her gaze found the man standing only a few feet away chatting with another lord. He smiled at her, and Sarah quickly looked away. She must give him no reason to get his hopes up.

"I find I wish to return to our cottage, Hammy."

"So soon? What will everyone say?"

Sarah rose from her seat. "If you wish to stay, I understand."

"Would you mind terribly?" Her companion's interest traveled across the room to a man standing close to the orchestra.

"Hammy?" Sarah sat down again. "In all the years we have been together...are you staring at that tall gentleman?"

"With the red hair?"

"Yes, Hammy."

Hammy cast her gaze downward, blushing. "He is an old family friend, nothing more."

A soft smile came to Sarah, and she grasped Hammy's hand. "Please, stay. Enjoy yourself. I shall walk back with Jenny and her brother. I see they are about to leave, too"

Hammy nodded and squeezed Sarah's hand affectionately. "I will not be too long."

Sarah delighted in the idea of her companion finding happiness, maybe even love. It was more than she could ever hope for. She decided to forget about Jenny or even collecting her wrap as she hurried out the front doors of the inn, descended the steps, walked silently past the collection of servants awaiting their masters inside, and up the street.

But before she crossed the road, she heard a man say, "I am afraid he will find out who you really are, Your Grace."

"Nonsense," a familiar, feminine voice said. "Coincidences do happen in real life. So we share the same solicitor…"

"And the same first name as his *mother*?"

"Well…" Lady Whitmore sighed. "There is that. But why did you tell him he could only rent the property when I already offered to sell it to him outright? He will think me addle-minded, if not worse. You must sell the Duke of Vexen the cottage and acreage immediately."

"Yes, Your Grace. And what name shall I affix to the deed of sale?"

She cleared her throat. "Are you purposely being impertinent?"

"Never." The man bowed. "Forgive my tone and manner, Your Grace. It has been a long day— and delicate plans of this nature are rather trying for a man of my age."

"I pay you too much to be troubled."

Sarah felt guilty for overhearing this very private conversation. She hadn't intended to encounter anyone. The walk to her cottage… *Dear God.* Even Lady Whitmore, who seemed to really be a duchess, held secrets. Big secrets, at that. And if she had heard correctly, the Duke of Vexen was her… No, she wouldn't dare think it. She turned her head and ran across the street as quietly as she could.

If they didn't see her, they'd never know

someone had overheard their conversation. Her hostess deserved all of the same discretion she demanded for all of her guests. Anonymity kept the small town of Whitmore productive and thriving. Sarah would never betray it.

As she reached the narrow path that cut through the woods, she stared up at the moon and stars, which were exceptionally bright tonight. "If I wish upon a star…"

"What exactly would you wish for?" The duke materialized from the shadows.

Sarah let out a little cry, holding her hand to her chest. "You must never do that to me again!"

He reached for her, but she stepped beyond his grasp.

"Sarah?"

"Miss Sarah," she insisted.

His grin grew wider. "Miss Sarah."

"Yes, Your Grace?"

"Are we back to playing our game?"

She frowned at him. "I have no idea to what you are referring, sir."

"Did I tell you how lovely you look in the moonlight?"

She waved her gloved hand dismissively. "Do not try to flatter me, Your Grace. Save it for Lady Loxley, or whatever female you are paying attention to at the moment."

"Ah," he said quietly. "Maria's plan was successful, I see."

"Plan?"

"Yes. She compelled me into the alcove, threw herself on me, and, I believe, hoped you would see us in a compromising position."

Oh! What an insufferable, self-righteous... She glanced away, ashamed she had thought the worst of him. Yet, she must never admit it. She shrugged. "And if I did?"

He successfully caught a lock of her hair between his fingers. "You are jealous."

"Don't be ridiculous!"

Could his grin grow any wider? More smug?

"Do you deny it, Sarah?"

She tipped her head up. "So are you."

"I never denied it." He caught her in his arms, holding her tightly to him. His heady smell, sandalwood and smoke, made her squirm. His warmth and hardness, strength and masculinity, it overwhelmed her, even frightened her at times like this. She could never deny him anything if he held her for too long.

"Let me go."

He snorted. "I could demand the same of you!"

"What could you possibly mean by that?"

He released her, only to step back a foot and stare at her intently. "Not in the physical sense, sweeting."

Was he implying she had a hold on his heart? "Why did you follow me?"

"Because you lack the instinct of self-preservation to be properly escorted home in the dark."

Now it was her turn to laugh. "And you are that sort of man?"

"Do you mock me?" His arm slipped about her waist, and he gave her a gentle shake.

Just as the immature girl in the tree would have done two years ago, she stuck her tongue out at him.

It must have caught Leonard by surprise, for he let her go and a deep-bellied bellow escaped him. "I believe..." he started, "that you are in desperate need of corporal punishment, Lady Sarah."

He meant to spank her like a child? The thought did not resonate well with her, and she backed up to a tree to protect her posterior. A lapse in judgement, for he prowled over to her, placed his hands on either side of her face, and leaned in, showering her with the lightest of kisses, first her nose, cheeks, earlobes, then her lips.

Her breath hitched, and she could not look away from his perfect features. Those wide eyes, full lips, his strong jaw. *Kiss me*, she begged silently, *a real kiss*.

"Sweeting," he whispered, "you are a temptress."

His mouth claimed hers for the briefest moment, his tongue sweeping over hers, demanding and sweet, but then he pulled away. She was left wanting more—leaning into him, one hand resting against his chest, the other gripping the material of his great coat.

Why couldn't he just sweep away all of her fears now, assure her he wanted her as wife, as his lover, as his everything?

"W-why did you stop?" she asked.

"The next time we kiss, Sarah, it will be because you cannot keep your delectable lips from mine."

CHAPTER ELEVEN

L EONARD'S WORDS ECHOED in her mind as she fell asleep that night, and they were still there the following morning. Since she was fairly sure he loved her, she could end this now with a kiss… Only it went against the grain to let him win.

Waiting for her at breakfast was a letter from her mother that made her squeak. "Hammy, my parents are coming to Whitmore!"

"How lovely," Hammy said distractedly.

Sarah raised her eyes to her old governess's tranquil face. "Hammy? Am I to understand you spoke to your—er—old family friend last night? The elegant gentleman with the red hair?"

"Indeed. He is most interested in classical poetry," Hammy said blushing. "We had an animated discussion, and he has offered to let me read his own poetry."

"I hope it's good," Sarah remarked, "for you

are quite a connoisseur."

"Well, it always used to be rather good, and I imagine he has only improved. Why—" She broke off, flustered when she saw Sarah smiling. She coughed. "Well, I shall let you know." She frowned suddenly. "Who did you say was coming to Whitmore?"

"My parents!"

Hammy beamed. "Well that is good news, is it not?"

"I don't know," Sarah said, thinking wildly of her reprehensible "game" with the duke, which, one way or another, her parents would put a stop to.

"I suspect they have heard of your wonderful singing," Hammy said. "And have come to hear. Lady Whitmore said something about a soiree at the castle. Something to do with the duke's excavations. Is not Lord Drimmen interested in antiquities?"

"Yes, but he does not get his hands dirty with digging them up."

"Well, he won't have to at a soiree," Hammy said reasonably. "They will just admire and discuss the history, and I'm sure you will be asked to sing at some point."

"Another exhibit," Sarah said with a curl of her lip.

"Is that not what you wanted? To be the exhibit your parents wanted to display? Only better than they could ever have imagined?"

She wrinkled her nose. "I wanted them to miss the old Sarah."

"She is still there, my dear. She has just lost her rough edges."

"And if I am still not good enough for them?"

"I think," Hammy said slowly, "that Lady Whitmore would rephrase the question as, are you good enough for *you*? Do you live up to your own expectations?"

"I don't know anymore. The whole basis of my expectations is crumbling…"

After breakfast, as they prepared to walk up to the castle with news of the Merringtons' visit, a morning caller was announced. Dangling her hat by its ribbon, Sarah tripped downstairs with a fast-beating heart, hoping it was the duke.

But when she entered the parlor, Hammy was greeting the tall, red-haired gentleman from last night. Which was almost as good.

"Sarah, this is Mr. Granville," Hammy said, her face flushed. "An old friend of my family's. Sir, my young friend, Miss Sarah, of whom I spoke yesterday evening."

Mr. Granville smiled and bowed over Sarah's extended hand.

"Shall I send for tea?" Sarah asked Hammy.

"Oh, but you are dressed to go out," Mr. Granville said.

"We can go any time," Sarah said.

Sarah stayed only long enough to discover that she liked the quiet, scholarly Mr. Granville, and that he appeared to be as humbly delighted with Hammy as the governess was with him. Making an excuse and promising to be back momentarily, she tied on her bonnet and departed, smiling. She had no intention of going back until Hammy had read *all* of his poems.

Although she set off for the castle and tried her best not to stray along the path to Leonard's excavation, she could not resist. Of course, he saw her and ran up to meet her, smiling almost as smugly as he had last night.

Well, two could play that game.

"Ah, have you come to lose your bet, Your Grace?"

The faintest flicker in his eyes betrayed his surprise, but he merely replied, "No, I have come to escort you. Again."

Color crept into her cheeks, but she held up one hand. "Then keep your distance, now that I know what your escort consists of."

"Come, now," he said, holding her gaze as they walked side by side, "don't you want to kiss me?"

She pretended to consider. "Yes," she admitted. "But I want to win more."

His fingers brushed hers, deliberately finding their way inside the cuff of her kid gloves and stroking. "Are you sure?"

"Oh yes," she said carelessly.

It was, she well knew, a challenge he could not resist. But quicker than she had bargained for, he tugged her off the path and behind the broad oak close by. He held her against him, his hands resting on her hips, his gaze on her lips.

"I don't believe you," he said huskily.

She arched one brow. "Do you accuse me of lying, Your Grace?"

"Leo," he breathed.

"Do you accuse me of lying, *Leo*," she said obediently.

"Yes, I do," he said softly. "What can it hurt? One kiss, and I promise it will not feel like losing."

His hands rested on her hips. He smelled of earth and the fresh sweat of recent labor. His lips hovered so close to hers, she could taste his breath. Her pulses racing, her whole being enveloped in heat, she had never been so tempted to close that tiny distance, to brush her mouth over his and cling. Desire was heady and made it impossible to think or hold on to a plan.

But surely, she was made of sterner stuff.

"I do not feel like losing," she said, albeit not quite steadily. "Do you really want me to kiss you?"

"You know I do."

"Why? To win?"

"Yes," he admitted. "But mainly to feel your

lips on mine, to know you want me as I want you."

"*You* may kiss *me* if you wish," she offered. *Oh yes, please kiss me, do it now...*

His lips curved, and she found herself fascinated by their texture.

"I said last night, the next kiss must come from you."

She came a fraction of an inch closer. "Then ask me to marry you," she whispered. "And I *will* kiss you."

His eyes only clouded further, like some tense, summer storm. "Kiss me and then I will ask."

"Oh dear," she said breathlessly. "It seems we are at an impasse. Let me know when you are ready to break it."

He groaned. "Sarah, you are a minx."

"Then what are you?"

"Desperate," he said frankly.

With a breath of laughter, she slipped out of his arms and walked on. She turned to wave back at him as he stood now on the path side of the oak. "Let me know when you wish to talk!"

"ARE YOU RESPONSIBLE for Hammy's Mr. Granville?" Sarah asked Lady Whitmore.

"If you mean for inviting him here, then yes. She mentioned a man from whom she had parted when young, because neither had a feather to fly with. I made a few inquiries."

"Thank you," Sarah said warmly. "I believe it might answer very well. I left them reading poetry together. He is not married, is he?"

"Not even widowed. I believe he always carried a torch for your Hammy, even when he inherited a modest fortune from an uncle and several caps were set at him."

"Hmm." Doubts assailed Sarah. "Should he not then have had the gumption to find her?"

"I expect there was family interference," Lady Whitmore said discreetly. "And then time, you know, runs away from us."

"You are very good," Sarah said curiously. "You are helping all of us all the time." Remembering the odd conversation she had overheard last night, she added, "If there is anything I can ever do to help you, you must tell me."

"I will," Lady Whitmore replied with a sweet smile. "In fact, it would help me considerably if you would make up the quarrel with your parents."

"Ah," she said frowning. "You invited them, too."

"Guilty as charged. But seriously, you must reach an understanding with them, for all your sakes."

"Leo, that is the duke, said something similar."

"Did he?"

Was that a trace of wistfulness in Lady Whitmore's voice?

"He said he would give anything for just one hour in the company of his late parents."

Lady Whitmore stood with unexpected speed. "He is a sweet boy." Her voice was not entirely steady.

Sarah said, "I never thought of him as sweet."

"I think you have. I also think it's time you admitted to your feelings."

"We have. Mostly. Not quite jokingly."

Lady Whitmore turned back, her eyes narrowed. "Are you still trying to defeat him?"

"Partly."

"Oh, don't throw him away, Sarah. He loves you."

Sarah couldn't deny the flood of pleasure at hearing the words, though she immediately demanded, "How do you know?"

Lady Whitmore's lips parted and then closed again. "I know," she said firmly. "Will you sing at my soiree when your parents are here?"

"Of course. Though I warn you, my voice will probably crack, and it will all go horribly wrong."

"I see no reason why it should. You sang beautifully for His Grace. Several times. Settle things, my dear. Don't leave yourself with all these unnecessary anxieties."

It was sound advice, but as it happened, she did not see the duke for several days. She wondered if he had finally lost interest in her, or if he was still playing the game, waiting for her to crack first.

CHAPTER TWELVE

M R. JAMES HAD arranged for a private meeting between the duke and his solicitor, Jenkins. A necessary distraction from the pleasantries of excavation and pursuing Lady Sarah. But hard facts had come to light that Leonard could no longer ignore after his fastidious secretary had done a deeper investigation about the cottage and land that Lady Whitmore had agreed to sell him only days ago, then unexpectedly offered to lease to him.

All three men sat at a table in the cabin the duke hoped to make his own soon, staring at each other in silence, the solicitor looking like he wished to be anywhere else.

"I want answers, Jenkins," Leonard demanded.

"Of course, Your Grace." The man's eyes clouded over with something akin to fear.

"How many years have you handled my

personal affairs?"

"Since the death of the late duke, Your Grace. And before that, I was privileged to serve your father for twenty years, if not more."

Leonard nodded and rubbed his chin, considering the small-statured man. He wanted to give him the benefit of the doubt, but Mr. James assured him there was life-altering news to be shared by the solicitor.

"I did not summon you here to play whist," the duke said. "Why the sudden change in terms for the property?"

Mr. Jenkins shook his head. "I am not at liberty to say."

"But you are, sir," Mr. James interjected. "I warned you that I have conducted my own investigation, including the baptismal records and marriage records at the church in nearby Chelton. Lady Whitmore is not who she appears to be, is she?"

The solicitor glanced at Mr, James, then stared at the duke. "I am within my rights to declare a conflict of interest between myself and yours and Lady Whitmore's personal business. Perhaps I can direct you to another solicitor within my firm to handle your future endeavors?"

Leonard smacked his open hand on the table, hoping to intimidate the stubborn man. "One way or another, Mr. Jenkins, I will have my answers—even if it means tossing you about first."

The solicitor reached for his cravat and seemed to loosen it some to breathe easier, his face splotched red. "Your Grace, such threats are unnecessary, I assure you."

"What are the chances of Lady Whitmore and His Grace sharing a solicitor?" Mr. James asked. "And what are the chances of our gracious hostess having the same first name as the duke's dearly departed mother?"

"Julia is a common enough name," Mr. Jenkins said quietly.

"Lady Whitmore is a widow. Has an estranged son who resides mostly in London. His name is..."

"Please, Mr. James." The solicitor shot up from his seat and started pacing. "Giving voice to such facts could start a scandal."

"Why?" Leonard asked.

"Whitmore is a special place, as you know, Your Grace. The lady invested all her time and money to make it what it is today—a sanctuary for lost souls."

"I am aware of her charitable acts. I approve deeply and wish to help support her causes, actually."

Mr. Jenkins managed to stop and offer the duke a weak smile. "She is an extraordinary woman."

"Yes."

"Some people do not wish to be found, sir."

Yes, Leonard had considered that when he and Mr. James had discussed some of his findings from the investigation—however… He gazed at his secretary, really his friend if Society allowed it, and nodded once, giving Mr. James permission to proceed.

"Frankly, Mr. Jenkins, His Grace believes it would serve a greater purpose to find out if Lady Whitmore is indeed the Dowager Duchess of Vexen."

"Hellfire…" the man said, not apologetic for cursing. "Would you bring down the House of Whitmore simply to satisfy your need for a mother?"

Leonard stood abruptly. "You forget to whom you speak, Mr. Jenkins."

"I do not!" The smaller man had a temper. "It is for her I speak, sir."

Leonard's contempt eased. "Why does she need such protection?"

"A lack of discretion over thirty years ago cost her more than any woman should have to pay for love."

"Love?" The duke swallowed the word, rolled it around inside his overworked mind, knowing what it felt like to love—to want—to need someone so bad it inspired one to break all the rules. "Tell me everything."

"Her marriage was not a love match, sir, far

from it. The duke, your father, was owed a great debt from Lady Whitmore's father, Lord Fordenham, and in order to protect his holdings, he gave the duke first choice in marrying one of his three daughters. Julia—Lady Whitmore—was beautiful, intelligent, and spirited—the type of woman any man would want. The duke chose her, though she had been secretly engaged for a year to Lord Redding, the son of a Spanish prince and grandson to the Marquess of Sedwick."

Leonard's heart raced, his hands fisted at his sides. "Continue, sir."

"Lady Whitmore adored her father and would do anything to please him and to keep her family safe. She married the duke, but after she gave birth to her son, she could no longer live the life she had been forced into and fled with Lord Redding to Spain. For six years they lived in banishment from England, but in love and happiness before he died tragically of consumption."

"Did they…" Leonard could not say it, could not ask if his mother had given birth to a bastard.

"Children?"

The duke nodded.

"Yes, a daughter."

"I… I have a sister?" The news hit him so hard, he was forced to sit down again. "Where is she?"

"France."

Leonard gazed at Mr. James. "Whatever it takes, find her and bring her home."

"Your Grace," the solicitor said, "have you considered the consequences of putting your own needs ahead of Lady Whitmore's?"

"You will refer to her as my mother, Her Grace, the dowager Duchess of Vexen, when in my presence."

"Yes—your mother."

"I have not had the time to think about anything critically, Mr. Jenkins, except that your services are no longer required by me. You played both sides of the cards, so to speak, and I am most disgusted by your ability to do so."

"But..." he sputtered.

"Do not worry, Mr. Jenkins, your livelihood is not in danger. I will handle this situation with utmost discretion. However, you will not receive a letter of recommendation from me, and I am sure your firm will wonder why they have lost one of their best clients."

"The firm was paid handsomely to keep this secret, Your Grace."

That made Leonard growl. "Get out before I change my mind and break you in half."

The solicitor grabbed up his leather satchel in haste and rushed out of the cottage, leaving Leonard in a fog of anger and wonder. He had a living, breathing mother. A sister. And a woman he wanted to marry. Damn his luck—nothing worth having was ever easy.

AFTER A LONG silence, James made one effort to speak. "Mr. Jenkins would actually be the best assistant in finding your sister."

Leonard sprang to his feet, gesturing dismissal with one hand. He didn't want to storm out of the castle, but suddenly he could not breathe. He could not yet debate whether or not he had behaved badly, whether or not his parents had. He just needed fresh air and solitude to absorb everything he had learned.

As he strode across the hall to the front door, he was vaguely aware of Lady Whitmore—his mother, the duchess—hovering, waiting. He could not speak to her, not now. He pretended not to see her and walked straight outside into the rain.

Thank God they had covered the pits at his digging site. But even for this, he could spare no focused thought. He pounded across the countryside, even breaking into a run, as though the exercise could expel the emotions tearing him apart.

Panting for breath, dripping wet, he skirted the village, realizing at last what an odd figure he would present to any observers. But it seemed his feet knew where to go, for he soon found himself in the lane that ran behind Sarah's cottage.

Only at the back gate did he hesitate. Instinct had drawn him here, but he was in no state to make morning calls, let alone continue their ridiculous game. And yet, his feet led him on to the kitchen door, where he rapped loudly.

The maid would send him about his business. In fact, she would probably scream.

The door flew open, and Sarah stood there, her eyes widening in astonishment.

"Leo!" Without hesitation, she threw the door wide, even reached out to grasp his arm and draw his sopping person inside. "What is it?" she demanded as he stood still, dripping on her kitchen floor.

He swallowed. "I'm sorry. I shouldn't have come, not like this." He turned toward the door, but she caught his hand, drawing him further into the kitchen toward the fire.

A maid gawped at him from the table, which she was scrubbing clean.

"Leave that just now," Sarah told her. "I'll watch the cakes while you clean the parlor before Miss Hammy returns."

Dragging her heels somewhat—no doubt from sheer curiosity—the maid left the kitchen.

Sarah was helping him out of his coat, which she hung on a hook near the fire, and gently pushed him onto the stool before it. She brought him a towel to dry his face and hair, and placed a cup of steaming tea on the hearth. Then she knelt, facing him and waited.

God, she was beautiful, never more so than with a smut of flour on her cheek, an apron over her fashionable morning gown, and her eyes full not of teasing or seduction or laughter, but of sheer concern.

He had never intended to come before her so vulnerable, emotionally naked. She could annihilate him with a word, ruin forever whatever advantage he had in this game which was so much more. *If I lose her now…*

She lifted the tea cup from the hearth, thrusting it into his hands. Obediently, he drank.

"I'm sorry," he managed. "I got caught in the rain."

A spark of humor lit her eyes, though it was kind. "Did you?"

He let out a breath of laughter. "I must look like a scarecrow after a storm."

"Are you well?"

He nodded.

"Then has something happened?"

Her gaze held his so that he could not look away. He opened his mouth, unsure what would come out. Then he closed it again and swallowed. "Lady Whitmore is my mother."

She waited, with so little reaction that he wondered if she had heard him, if he had spoken the words only in his head.

Then the truth hit him. "You knew!" A bitter laugh tore from him. "Even you!"

"What do you mean, *even me?*" she demanded.

He sprang up from the stool. "My father lied to me, telling me she was dead. Everyone else, family, friends, old servants, tenants, solicitors, have deliberately kept the truth from me. All my life! And now I discover *you*..."

"I accidentally overheard a private conversation of Lady Whitmore's," Sarah interrupted. "It led me to suspect, but I knew nothing. Here, privacy is respected, remember? Besides, I thought you knew. I thought that was why you were here." She reached for his hand, tugging him back down onto the stool.

He let her, even clung to her hand.

After a moment, she said, "Are you not pleased? You told me once what you would give just to speak to your parents."

Emotion surged, swamping him. "Of course I am pleased. She is a wonderful... I never dreamed... It's the *lies*, the deceit that tear me apart. And the sordid scandal that surrounds it all!"

And then, of course, it came tumbling out, all that Jenkins had told him about his mother's lover and her other child. "She left me," he blurted at the end. "For *him*."

Sarah reached up, tenderly brushing the damp hair from his forehead. "Sordid scandal," she repeated. "Have you considered that is why she left you? To keep you from it? Besides, love is never sordid. You cannot know the circumstances that decided her to go, but I do know it broke her heart. It is not a decision she can have made lightly. And yet she still keeps you from the scandal."

He stared at her, catching her hand against his cheek. "Why did she bring me here?"

Sarah smiled. "I thought it was for me. But perhaps it was always for her. Leo, imagine your hurt, and double it, triple it, multiply it by hundreds—that is what she is feeling. What she has felt for a quarter of a century. In a funny way, I believe this—Whitmore, all her charity—is for you. It's more than atonement. It's her gift to all of us, but chiefly to you."

He searched her face, for some reason liking the words, though he would need to mull them. He released her hand and drank his tea thoughtfully. Gradually, the warmth from the fire seeped into his bones, along with the beginnings of peace. He had never seen Sarah as peaceful before. Desirable, fascinating, enchanting, but definitely chaotic. There was more to her. There was more to everyone than the world ever saw.

He rose, and set his cup on the table, then returned to take his still damp coat from the hook, and struggle into it.

She had risen with him and now stood watching him.

He took both her hands. "Thank you."

"For what?"

"Everything." He raised her hands to his lips, and kissed them both. "Goodbye."

SARAH WATCHED HIM go with something like wonder. It seemed he could always surprise her. From the confident, seductive man she had last encountered, oozing masculine charm and persuasion, to this lost, vulnerable boy who had just left her.

A smile playing on her lips, she pressed her hands to her cheeks, as though she could feel more closely the places he had kissed.

"Oh, I do love you," she whispered wistfully.

And he had come to her in his moment of agony. She didn't know whether it meant neither of them could win their foolish game. Or if both had already won.

CHAPTER THIRTEEN

I T WAS ALMOST teatime when Leonard finally entered the castle library. Part of him had hoped his mother would summon him, take the lead in this inevitable encounter. But Leonard, fifth Duke of Vexen, had never shirked a challenge. And although his heart beat like a schoolboy's before his headmaster, he sought her out because he suspected she would never presume. Would she have just carried on treating him like an honored guest? Pretending neither of them knew the truth of their relationship?

As he walked into the library, Miss Frobe all but scuttled out, like a ghost, apart from the quick, nervous smile she cast him. Leonard remembered to bow.

Lady Whitmore, his mother, was alone at her usual desk. She rose as he approached, but said nothing. Her expression gave little away, and she stood straight and proud as ever. And yet something in her stillness spoke of tension. Perhaps, she, too, was held together by a thread. Perhaps she was afraid.

With the thought, he bit back the accusation on the tip of his tongue and instead blurted, "Why? Make me understand."

"Oh, Leonard," she sighed. "What can I say that you will believe? That I was young and foolish and should never have allowed myself to be married to your father? That I cannot regret it because our union gave birth to you? That when he found out I had seen Ferdinand again, he kept you from me? That it broke my heart to leave you, but I did it anyway? That I came home to England because of you? It is all true, and yet none of it is relevant now."

He stared. "Not *relevant*?"

"No, for it is past and cannot be undone. Regrets, recriminations, defense—they mean nothing against the fact that you and I are here under the same roof, that we have begun to know each other a little at last."

He tugged at his cravat, fighting the bitterness. "You have been here some fifteen years. Don't pretend you came home for my sake."

"But I did. I would not ruin your life with my continued existence. I knew everyone believed I was dead. But here, I could more easily get news of you. And when I spoke to Sarah... I could not resist inviting you here to see the man you had become."

He spun away from her. "You would have me believe my father was so cruel, so deceitful."

"No," she said wearily. "Your father was a good man. I hurt him. He hurt me. And then, I suppose, he was protecting you from scandal. I have discovered there is no point in regretting mistakes, only learning from experience."

He swung back to face her, frowning. Natural courtesy reasserted itself as he realized she still stood. He took her hand—it felt frail in his fingers and trembled—and conducted her to the sofa. He sat beside her, half-turned toward her.

"What is Sarah's part in this?" he demanded.

"None. I sensed great feeling in her. For you. I set out to discover if she was worthy of you, and then I brought you here to see what would happen." Her gaze fell to the fingers clasped in her lap. "And to see you."

He drew in his breath. "This is madness. At the age of eight-and-twenty, I suddenly have a mother. What do I call you? Mama? Your Grace?"

"I thought we had already decided on Julia, in private. Lady Whitmore in public."

"But there *is* no Lady Whitmore. Only a Duchess of Vexen."

She shook her head. "The disgraced duchess is dead. I am Lady Whitmore."

He was frowning again. "No. You must come home and take your rightful place. Honor demands it."

She smiled. "Whose honor, Leonard? My dear, I will not rake up old scandal again. My place is here in a life I love. And there will be a new duchess soon enough."

If she sought to distract him with that implication, it failed. He did not give up so easily, but he saved the fight for later, instead saying, "I understand I have a sister."

She inclined her head. "Ferdinand's daughter."

"Where is she?" he asked. "Did you abandon her, too?" He regretted it almost at once, for her pale cheeks whitened further. "Forgive me," he muttered. "But I need to find my sister. Where is she?"

"I'm afraid I cannot tell you. It is up to her to make herself known if she wishes it."

"Why is everything such a damnable secret?" he burst out. "Do I not have the right to know my sister? To know that she is safe and cared for?"

"She is. As for the rest, you must be patient. The world, Leo, does not revolve around only *your* needs."

"So, I'm beginning to discover," he said grimly.

"It is not meant to punish you, but to protect her. If she reveals herself, do you not realize she, too, will have to face the scandal of being a by-blow?"

"Mother!" It came out so naturally, if not uneasily, that Leonard surprised himself. "Lady Whitmore," he quickly corrected, "I am astonished that such words would come out of your mouth."

"Not my words," she said. "Society's very own term for such an unfortunate child. Would bastard be more suitable?"

If he could, the duke would rip his hair out strand by strand to ease the building pressure in his chest. He paced away from her, stared out the mullioned windows, then walked back to her. "We can never return to the lives we were leading just twenty minutes ago. We are bound by more than just honor... Blood."

"Yes," she agreed, renewed strength in her voice. "Whether I am Lady Whitmore or a long-forgotten duchess, makes no difference. I am still your mother, am I not?"

Irritation rose inside him, knowing he'd spend countless nights awake, wondering what his life would have been like if he'd had her in it. It made no difference really, not if common sense, of which he had copious amounts, ruled his heart. He must accept the facts of his old life and the change in the one moving forward. There must be a way to join the two, to find peace for everyone involved. The one thing he did know... "I will never allow you to leave me again." That decision was non-negotiable as he stared down at her, in awe and tender feelings.

Tears wet the corners of her eyes, and she sniffled. "I would expect nothing less from my son." She reached her hand out, and he took it immediately, dropping to his knee in front of her, kissing her knuckles, and bowing his head.

"I have waited a lifetime for this," he said, choking on his words. "Have seen your sweet face a thousand times in my dreams. Father never spoke of you. Often times I begged for information about you, wanting to know you as any boy would wish to get close to his deceased mother, but he forbade it. Only one thing remained…"

"Yes?" She rested her hand on the top of his head, and Leonard gazed up at her.

He slowly climbed to his feet, reached inside his coat, and pulled out a small, oval-shaped locket. "This." He offered it to her.

She took it and opened it to reveal a miniature painting of herself on one side, and Leonard's likeness as a child on the other. Her mouth fell open as she glanced up at him. "He let you keep this?"

"Yes."

"This was a gift for my birthday from your father. Before I left, I set this by your bedside. Perhaps your father had a soft side after all." She closed the locket and handed it back to him. "The image of your dear face has never left me, Leonard. Never."

"I must ask…" he hesitated.

"Ask me anything, you deserve what answers I can give."

"No."

"Please."

He turned away, took a fortifying breath, then faced her again. "Why didn't you keep a lover, like so many wedded men and women do?"

She did not seem embarrassed or offended by the question. "I could never masquerade as a loving wife and mother, then spend my nights in the bed of another. I am afraid it was all or nothing for me. I tried so hard to keep my feelings hidden, to squelch the fire burning inside of me." She sighed. "I failed miserably, as you know. That is why I left, Leonard, to find love and happiness and to give you a chance at a respectable life."

Their hands found each other again, holding on for dear life. "I cannot promise that living this lie, pretending you do not exist, will be palatable to me," he said. "You are my mother, and though scandal would shake the pillars of Vexen, I do not care what the world thinks."

"Do not make a hasty decision, Your Grace," she said, suddenly withdrawing her hands from his, taking on the air of formality.

Leonard looked up and found Maria and

Lord Trenton standing in the doorway, watching them.

"Has something happened?" Maria asked, entering the room with her usual rudeness.

"Nothing that would interest you," the duke said smugly.

"Your Grace," she said, slinking up beside him and taking his arm, "don't you know by now that *anything* that happens is of interest to me?"

Wishing he could shake her off violently and forget he had ever formed an attachment with her in the past made him growl. Honor demanded he play a certain role when in company of others, but the moment he got her alone…

"I believe you promised to take a walk with me today, Your Grace."

Lady Whitmore nodded her approval. "I have afternoon appointments."

"Very well," Leonard said. "I will be delighted to show you and Lord Trenton my dig site."

"Dig site?" Maria seemed deeply disappointed by the prospect. "What interest would I have in mud and sand?"

"Give the old boy a chance to show us what he has found," Lord Trenton interjected. "I am more than curious."

"Vikings conquered this land long ago," Leonard offered. "The beach is filled with artifacts from the ninth and tenth centuries, I believe. Imagine what treasures will be donated to the London museums."

"That is all very well," Maria said in a huff. "But I am hardly dressed for such an outing, and my shoes…"

"If you wish to go and change, we will wait for you," Lord Trenton offered.

His suggestion made Maria smile wickedly. "Who am I to turn down such generosity?"

She rushed out of the room, and Leonard bowed to Lady Whitmore before he, too, found his way out.

"Your Grace!" Lord Trenton called.

"Yes?" He stopped and turned back to the gentleman.

"Will you not wait for Lady Maria?"

Leonard smiled. He'd not waste another moment on that meddlesome creature. "No," he said. "I am sure she is in capable hands."

Something overwhelmingly powerful ignited his blood, told him to return to Sarah's cottage— to hold her, gaze into her lovely eyes, to touch her everywhere, to breathe her in, to claim her for himself before it was too late.

Yes, claim her.

Make love to her if she wished it.

But would she?

Two unannounced visits to her home in one day? What would her maid say? What would her companion think? The duke did not give a damn. He opened the gate, strode up the cobbled walkway, and raised his hand to knock on the door, but it opened before he got the chance.

Sarah stood before him, her hair down and damp, wearing a silk wrap...she had obviously just taken a bath. Heat surged through his body, molten and dangerous. He raked his gaze over her, from her trim ankles to her thick, unruly curls, dark and beautiful. The scent of roses reached him, and before she could say anything, he pressed her inside, shut the door behind them, and kissed her like he never had before—pressing his hard length against her.

"Leonard..." she breathed out.

"Sarah, my Sarah at that." He kissed her again, his tongue finding solace in her sweet mouth, tasting and taking what he needed to calm his bedeviled soul. "I want you, Sarah, more than I've ever wanted anyone in my life."

She threaded her arms around his neck, pressing her soft breasts against his chest. "I want you, Leonard, whatever that entails..."

Hesitation hit him as he looked about. "Where is your maid? Where is Hammy?"

"G-gone for the afternoon. Both," she whispered, kissing him again.

He nodded in relief, grateful for the rare gift of privacy. All he knew in the moment, he must rid them both of the barriers of material between them. His eyes, his hands, even his heart, longed to see her naked, to finally breathe in every inch of her delicate, creamy skin. He scooped her into his arms, breathing out a ragged breath.

"Your chamber?"

She rested her head against his chest, unresponsive.

"Sarah."

She raised her head. "Yes?"

"Your chamber, sweeting."

She pointed to the stairs.

Leonard rushed up and along the narrow corridor and, when she indicated, pushed the door open with his foot. A canopied bed awaited them.

"Mine at last," he said, stepping inside and closing the door.

"Your Grace," she said demurely, staring up at him.

"Yes, sweeting?"

"I do believe you have lost our wager."

CHAPTER FOURTEEN

A T LEAST IT gave him pause, allowed her a moment to actually think.

After his first stunned blink, warm amusement pierced the passion in his eyes. "How do you come to that conclusion?"

"Surely, you cannot mean to ravish me without at least a promise to marry?"

A wicked smile curved his sensual lips. "I *could* make you the offer now, but is there any point when *you* have already lost?"

Her eyes widened. "I?"

"You kissed me. In the hall, directly after you told me Hammy is not here. I concede that I participated fully, but the first impetus came from you."

"That does not count. It was a mere continuation of the kisses begun by you."

His laughter was warm as he took her face between his hands. "Are you saying that if I want the sweet pleasures of your body, I must make my offer first?"

It was, of course, exactly what she meant, but the words seemed to stick in her throat.

"You want me to go?" he asked gently.

Her breath caught. He meant it. If she asked, he would leave her. Without meaning to, she grasped his wrists, but staring into his heat-filled eyes was a mistake. They excited and consumed her, and she could not bear him to go. Mutely, she shook her head.

"Then you will have to marry me," he murmured.

"Is that your offer?" she asked shakily.

His lips were so close to hers, she could almost taste them. Her whole being ached for him.

"Oh, my sweet," he whispered. "I always meant to marry you. And now I'll never let you go."

Enchanted, she closed the tiny distance between them, and kissed him.

His lips smiled on hers, but only for an instant before he swept her up in his arms once more and strode to the bed.

When she landed on the pillows, her dressing gown had gone and she lay naked, her skin burning beneath his avid eyes. She plucked desperately at the covers, her first instinct being to hide herself, but Leo's reaction distracted her.

His hungry gaze devoured her. His breathing came in pants, and for the first time, she realized her power. Wondering, she stilled her fingers and let him look his fill. God help her, she liked him to look.

He tore off his coat, dropping it on the floor. His cravat, waistcoat, and shirt quickly followed. Her arms lifted of their own accord, summoning him, reaching for him. And nothing had ever felt so sweet and heady as his naked skin or hers. When he kissed her, more deeply than ever before, she was lost. Her body reacted on its own, arching up into him as her hands stroked his back and hips.

The heat building at the base of her stomach caught fire. Her whole body trembled with need, responding to his every caress and kiss, from her eyelids to her breasts and stomach and the inside of her thighs. She moaned when he found the center of her desire, and then he was inside her and she cried out.

He paused, staring down into her astonished eyes. Then he kissed her softly. "Only a moment's discomfort. Relax and move with me." His voice was hoarse. His whole body shook with the effort of restraint, which for some reason, allowed all her excitement to flood back. She obeyed him, with growing wonder, clung to him as passion drove them both to the heights of pleasure and ultimate joy.

SOMEWHERE, SHE COULD not quite believe that he lay naked in her arms, his head on her breasts, after loving her. No longer the child who had thrown apples at him and sought revenge for perceived insults, she was a woman at last. What they had done did not remotely shame or even embarrass her. She knew only wonder and delight and a wicked desire for more. She had loved the play of hard muscle under her caresses, gloried in the hard strength that yet showed her such tenderness, such soft, sensual pleasure.

Stroking his short, tousled hair, she realized he was smiling.

"What?" she asked.

"Nothing. I am just happy. My world was upside down, and now it is not only righted but wonderful." He raised his head. "I found great joy in you."

"And I in you," she whispered.

He kissed her then with great tenderness.

"Why now?" she asked. "Why did you come back?"

"I think I came to tell you I had reached some understanding with my mother. Partly. Mostly, I came just to see you, to hold you if I could. I didn't really expect this happiness, though I can't deny I hoped for it." His arms tightened around her. "I should not have so risked your reputation, but I cannot be sorry."

"Neither can I," she admitted.

"But I should go before your Hammy returns."

"Probably," she said reluctantly. "At least no one in the village will gossip if they saw you come in. That is one of the many beauties of Whitmore."

"I would not have the world think ill of you just because my ardor was too urgent." He dropped a kiss on her hair and sat up, dangling one long, muscular leg over the side of the bed.

Fresh desire curled in her stomach.

"When do your parents arrive?" he asked.

"Tomorrow. Before Lady Whitmore's soiree."

He nodded. "Then I will speak to your father when he arrives at the castle." Smiling, he leaned over and took her back into his arms. "I cannot quite believe in my own happiness. I will spend every day trying to make you just as happy as I... We shall have such fun, you and I."

She kissed him and pressed her cheek to his. She truly believed they would.

AS THEY WALKED together to the front door,

Leonard thought he would explode with the joy she had just given him, with excitement for a future spent with her. Life was suddenly wonderful. He felt as if there was nothing he could not do.

Beside him, Sarah was dressed modestly in a morning gown of pale blue, but her dark curls still spilled around her shoulders. She was so beautiful; he didn't know how to keep his hands off her. In a bid to try, he opened the front door.

But he could not leave her without one more kiss. Since a quick glance up the path to the street showed him no one, he wrapped her in his arms and kissed her thoroughly. She clung to him, responding with a passion that delighted him.

"My," drawled a voice from the gate. "What a sight to delight the gossips."

Leonard knew that voice only too well. Inwardly, he groaned. Outwardly, he refused to be hurried. Although Sarah's lips had stilled with shock and she made a quick flutter to be free, he deliberately finished the kiss, before releasing her.

"I'll deal with her," he breathed and stepped outside, closing the door on Sarah.

He strolled along the path toward Maria Loxley and a highly embarrassed Trenton. Of all the people who could have walked past Sarah's gate at that precise moment, it had to be these two strangers, unbound by the laws of privacy which governed Whitmore.

"Why, Leonard," Maria said, apparently amused although her eyes flashed with a quite different emotion. "I thought you were too much the gentleman to ruin unmarried, gently born young ladies."

"I am."

Maria laughed, "What, will you pretend it was the maid?"

"I shan't pretend anything at all," Leonard replied. "With respect, Maria, it is none of your business. As guests here, we must all abide by the rules. I am trusting your discretion, Trenton."

"Of course," Trenton said stiffly.

"Run along, my lord," Maria commanded. "His Grace will escort me to the inn, since it seems we have all lost interest in his muddy pits."

Trenton tipped his hat and stalked off. Ruefully, Leonard remembered that the young earl was interested in Sarah on his own account.

"What is it you want to say?" Leonard asked Maria bluntly as they walked toward the inn. "You had best get it over with, but I tell you now, I will not discuss the cottage I have just left or any who reside there."

"Well that limits the conversation," Maria observed. "But I suppose you need not discuss, just listen. I don't *know* who she is, but I am aware Lord Drimmen's daughter is here, and so I do *suspect*. I am prepared to believe you did not seduce her—frankly, I could more easily imagine the other way around—but my dear, the world will not believe that. Kissing at the front door with her hair loose about her shoulders? While no one else is at home? Yes, I met the companion in the square with that tediously serious red-haired man, so I know you were alone with Miss Sarah." She smiled. "What a tale that would make for the gossips."

"Don't, Maria, it is you who will look both foolish and ill-natured. You must know I mean to marry her."

Pain surged in her eyes, but before he could soften his tone, it was replaced by fury. Then her darkened lashes swept down, hiding her emotion.

"Oh, no, Leonard," she said in quite a different voice, hard and cruel. "You mean to marry *me.*"

"Maria, we have gone over this before. We did not suit as lovers. We most definitely would not suit as husband and wife."

"Duke and duchess," she mused. "I shall make an excellent duchess, regal, witty, the perfect hostess."

"Not with this duke," Leonard said firmly. "Let it go, Maria."

"Why, no, I couldn't do that. You asked for my discretion."

He frowned, uncomprehending.

"My discretion," she explained patiently, "will be assured for your—er—hand in marriage."

"Don't be ridiculous."

"Ridiculous?" she repeated, gazing at him

innocently. "You *want* me to speak to her parents? You know they will immediately take her home in a rage. If only they could find a nunnery, they would immure her in one. As it is, she will be buried in the country."

"Not if I offer for her," Leonard got out, forced by sheer fury into discussing what he had sworn not to. "I am not no one. Merrington will be glad to give her to me."

"But the world will laugh at her. The foolish chit who charmed you with a song, married from pity after a sordid scandal."

"No one would believe such idiocy," Leonard retorted.

"Oh, but they would," Maria said softly. "Trust me, I would see to it."

He stared at her. "Why?" he asked helplessly.

"Well, if I can't be a duchess—your duchess—I would have to have something else to amuse me. But don't despair, my darling. I know you will never let that happen. Announce our engagement tomorrow evening, and my wicked tongue is stilled. After that, I'm afraid your little songbird will be nothing but an object of scorn and ridicule. And just think—she will owe all that to you."

Without a word, Leonard swung away from her and strode across the square in the opposite direction. Her soft, mocking laughter followed him, and he acknowledged, savagely, that he deserved it.

CHAPTER FIFTEEN

SARAH COULD KEEP silent no longer—for she'd watched the confrontation between Maria and her beloved duke. Where that woman was concerned, no good could follow, and the way Leonard had stormed off... She secured her cloak about her shoulders and rushed off in the direction of the inn, counting on finding Maria alone. Since the day that woman appeared, she had done nothing but look down on Sarah and go out of her way to insult her, to treat her as a lesser being.

As she approached the cobbled walkway that lead to the inn, she spotted Maria lingering in the small gardens of to the side of the building. The widow appeared to be alone and talking to herself with a self-satisfied smile on her face.

"Are you looking for me, Miss Sarah?" she asked, barely gracing her with a look in her direction.

Sarah rolled her eyes. "Indeed, I am."

"How fortunate for you that I foresaw your need to speak with me. That's why I am out here."

Sarah entered the neatly laid out garden, admiring the different species of roses. There were two stone benches, and she sat down on one. "Why would you assume that I wanted to talk to you?"

Maria chuckled and faced her. "Perhaps it had something to do with that indiscretion in the front of your cottage."

"I hardly call a kiss an indiscretion, Lady Maria. It was a gesture of respectable affection between myself and my betrothed."

"Betrothed," she repeated sarcastically. "Is that what the duke told you? He's a rogue of the highest order, believe me."

Sarah had hoped to avoid hearing the sordid details about Leonard's dalliances with Maria, but the woman seemed determined to share her experiences. "Perhaps he was a rogue with you…"

Maria snorted rather unattractively. "Let me guess, you think you are special to him?"

"We were nearly betrothed three years ago."

"Oh, yes, I know the story well, for he sought comfort in my bed soon after his encounter with you—the other you, I mean."

"The other me?" she asked in a steely voice.

"Of course, the little hoyden who wouldn't know what to do with a duke if another woman showed her step by step."

The insult was meant to hurt Sarah, and it did, but she held her composure as she'd been taught to do. "Especially if that woman was you."

Maria frowned but remained indifferent, her air of superiority unaffected. "Give up the duke, my dear, he is too much for a girl like you to handle. Try for an earl. That I can help you with. Or even a baron. A country baron at that. You seem to flourish in this backwater environment, why not stay where you are comfortable and safe from the *ton*?"

Sarah rewarded her with a genuine smile. "I think you have already realized I am the daughter of an earl, more than your equal."

"In title only," Maria spat. "By getting caught kissing the duke, I have gained leverage over you, *Lady* Sarah. That gives me the power to make your life miserable if you give me reason to."

Sarah stood, taller than Maria by at least three inches. "Are you threatening me?"

Maria shrugged. "If you wish to call it that, who am I to disagree?"

"You don't even know me. Why would you wish to harm me?"

Maria gave her a serious look. "You got in my way."

"Are you admitting to coming to Whitmore

under false pretenses? Not to contribute to Lady Whitmore's charitable causes but to seduce a duke?"

Maria scowled. "I came here to do both. I admire Lady Whitmore sincerely. She is the kind of woman anyone would strive to be like."

"Except you."

Maria pretended to smooth her skirts. "What woman wouldn't pursue Leonard? He is a duke, after all. Wealthy. Handsome. Powerful."

"Honest. Intelligent. Honorable…"

"Oh, those qualities pale in comparison to what I adore about him. He can save honor for Parliament or whatever else he does with his time."

Her lack of caring for Leonard shocked Sarah. "You do not love him."

A furrow appeared between her brows. "Love? You are desperately naïve, Sarah. Perhaps your companion should stop reading you fairy tales when you retire at night. Love is for saints and children, not dukes and duchesses, not for a man like Leonard and a woman like me. Ours will be a union of mutual benefits. We will be the talk of Society. The handsomest couple in London, don't you think?"

The thought of such a woman bearing the title of Duchess of Vexen angered Sarah. "You are after his money. You care nothing about him."

"That is where you are mistaken, child. I care

very much about him. So much so that I am willing to marry him, give him an heir, and manage his affairs—that takes plenty of caring."

What could she say in response to that? Maria did not hide her intentions, and Leonard must know what she wanted from him. He practically ran any time the woman went near him. But she had not expected Maria to be so brazen about it all. "Perhaps we should let Leonard decide who he wants for a wife."

Maria clasped her hands together with delight. "That is a magnificent idea."

Disgusted, Sarah took her leave, heading back to her cottage—fear uncoiling inside her. What had Maria said to Leonard after he left her cottage? Unfortunately, she would have to wait, there were other things to worry about, for as she drew near her home, her mother, father, and Lady Whitmore were waiting for her outside.

>>>><<<<

"THE WOMAN IS calculating and cold, Mr. James, unworthy of anything respectable."

Mr. James sat quietly as Leonard continued to pace and talk.

"Can you believe she is attempting to blackmail me? Threatening to ruin my sweet Sarah?"

"Desperation is an ugly trait in a woman, sir."

"Quite right," the duke agreed.

"You have so much on your plate to contend with already," his secretary said. "Reunited with your long-lost mother, the dig site, a new property, and now a wife."

"Wife?"

"I presume you intend to marry Lady Sarah. Is that not the reason for all this upset?"

"You are peculiarly perceptive, Mr. James. Almost to the point of unsettling."

"I apologize, then. But is that not precisely why you hired me, Your Grace?"

Leonard gazed at him and cracked a smile. "It wasn't for your good looks."

Mr. James grinned. "There is only room for one dandy under your roof, sir."

Bloody hell—such disrespect. He laughed even harder. "Maria will play her game as brutally as a professional gambler with nothing left to lose."

Mr. James scratched his chin. "Shall I watch her for you, sir?"

"I think that would be helpful. But do not be obvious."

"Of course not. Discretion is my favorite thing, Your Grace."

Leonard waved him off and headed for the castle. He needed a hot bath and a change of clothes—perhaps a stiff drink or two to chase away the unease he felt inside. Sarah's beautiful face invaded his thoughts, then. The way she cried his name as he made love to her, her sweet smile and innocence, her need to please him though she had no experience with men. She was naturally curious and unafraid of his masculinity.

That pleased him immensely. So did the idea of a lifetime to explore passion with her and to teach her the secrets of the boudoir. His manhood throbbed with need. Just the thought of her excited him. But Maria... The pleasurable feeling withered quickly. That woman had been a selfish lover, lazy and spoiled by her former lovers. She never gave what she received—only...

He cursed himself for being so careless about Sarah, for kissing her outside the privacy of the cottage.

What had he been thinking?

Did he really want an answer to that ridiculous question?

No. Because he hadn't been thinking at all, only feeling.

How he loved her. Perhaps even on the day he met her in the tree...the kind of patient love that would grow into something deeper once she became a woman. There was no doubt about her ability to make him laugh or to entertain him. Her angelic voice would fill the rooms of Vexen Hall for the next fifty years.

He arrived at the castle and went immediately to his room and ordered his valet to fill his bathtub. He had to devise a way to keep Maria quiet without risking Sarah's reputation and her heart.

SARAH'S MOTHER LOOKED her over critically. "That dress is unbecoming to a lady of your standing."

Sarah gazed down at the soft blue fabric. She adored the walking dress. "It's brand new, Mother, made by the modiste here in Whitmore."

"I find it to be a clever design," Lady Whitmore said. "Sturdy material for the country, yet charming and very pretty."

Sarah's mother looked at Lady Whitmore. "I suppose when you put it like that, it is a fetching design."

"Not for London, though," Lady Whitmore offered.

"Indeed not," Sarah was forced to agree, disappointed to be on display, and even more hurt by her mother's criticism. "You will never guess who has been here the last week, Mother."

Lady Drimmen took a sip of her tea and then set the cup down. "Someone we should be concerned about?"

"Of course not," Lady Whitmore answered

for Sarah. "I'd consider him more than an old friend." She patted Sarah's hand.

Her mother did not try to guess. "You know I dislike surprises, Sarah."

"The Duke of Vexen," she said, trying to contain her enthusiasm.

Her mother's face tightened at the mention of his name. "That man..."

"Mother."

"Why is he always around to see the worst in you? God knows what he thinks of your eccentricities now he has found you in this place! How can you be pleased that His Grace is here to see you living in a *cottage*, without your family, wasting your time on obscure lectures and *public singing*, from all I can gather. If he was disgusted before, what must he think now?"

Disappointment filled Sarah's heart. She had thought her mother would be happy with her progress, the obvious change in her character. But nothing seemed to please the woman, *nothing*. The only good thing was that her father had taken a walk to stretch his legs after the long carriage ride. At least she'd be spared being humiliated in front of him.

"If I recall correctly," Lady Whitmore said, "the Duke of Vexen did not refuse Sarah, he just saw the wisdom in giving her time to mature into the woman she is now."

Lady Drimmen smiled weakly at their hostess. "Is that what Sarah told you?"

"Of course not," Lady Whitmore said. "The duke confided in me once he knew Lady Sarah was here."

Her mother glared at her. "It should have never been discussed. Though I respect His Grace as a member of the peerage, my personal feelings toward him are less than favorable. I'm sure you understand, Lady Whitmore."

Sarah's stomach felt queasy all of a sudden as she glanced at Lady Whitmore. How she could remain so calm while her mother insulted her son, she didn't know, but admired her for it. "Mother, the duke was perfectly right to put off our betrothal. I was not ready for marriage, much less to a duke."

"Nonsense. Marriage and the position of duchess, would have been the making of you."

Sarah sighed and lost herself in private thought, wondering where Leonard had got to—was he with Maria? Her hands trembled, but she hid them in the folds of her dress. Hopefully her father would be more receptive—more pleased with her transition from a spoiled child into a woman who was ready to get married and take her place in Society. A duchess...she'd never dreamed it possible after Leonard had put her off the first time. She smiled.

"Sarah?" her mother said in a chastising tone. "Why do you simper?"

"Simper?"

"Yes, you heard me correctly."

She shrugged. "I am happy, Mother."

"Happy? Whatever for?"

"To be here."

"Well, that is about to change, my dear."

Sarah cast her mother a wary glance. "Why? In what way?"

"Well, just as soon as we have recovered from our journey north, we shall journey south again to London. Your father has found a most eligible gentleman who might well be induced to offer for you."

I am already engaged to the duke! She bit back the frustrated retort, for after all, Leo wished first to speak to her father as was only proper. Still, this reunion with her mother was hardly going the way she had hoped.

"Who has he roped in now?" she asked lightly.

Her mother frowned at such levity. "Lord Greythorpe. A widower, it is true, but there were no children of his first marriage."

Sarah stared at her. "Greythorpe? But he is a friend of Papa's! He is old!"

"He is two-and-forty," her mother said tartly. "Hardly in his dotage! And it seems to your father and I that you will do better with an older man, who will sober you."

A wave of revulsion swept over Sarah. But

again, she swallowed back her anger. "We may discuss it further in London, if the matter arises," she said peaceably and was rewarded by Lady Whitmore's smile of approval.

The front door banged open and closed again, presumably Sarah's father retuned from his walk.

Lady Whitmore rose from her chair. "Ah, there is his lordship. Shall we return to the castle, Lady Drimmen? Sarah, we look forward to seeing you and Miss Hammy at tonight's soiree."

CHAPTER SIXTEEN

WHEN SARAH AND Hammy arrived at the castle, at least Lady Drimmen found nothing to criticize in her daughter's dress. Well, not beyond, "The gown needs jewels, garnets perhaps."

"I have little jewelery in Whitmore," Sarah replied.

"The simplicity suits you perfectly," Lady Whitmore assured her.

Across the room, Leonard stood by the table displaying the items he had dug up. He was in earnest conversation with a group of interested people, and Sarah's heart swelled. She would have liked to exchange smiles with him, just to give her courage, but he did not glance in her direction.

She moved instinctively toward him, but her mother, sounding shocked, said, "Sarah, you will stay by me."

Oh, yes, the world had intruded upon Whitmore, confining her in the ways she could never bear. At least as a married woman she would have freedom to walk across a room to speak to whomever she chose.

As Sarah stood restlessly beside her mother, even Hammy, with a small, apologetic smile, escaped across the room to her Mr. Granville. Examining the objects on Leonard's table, his face lit up in a spontaneous smile as she approached, and he walked forward to meet her.

"Does Miss Hammond usually put herself forward in such a manner?" her mother asked disapprovingly.

"She is greeting an old friend, Mother," Sarah said patiently. "She hardly needs to play duenna when you are here." She turned to smile at her friend Jenny and Jenny's brother Charles, and present them to her mother.

For a few minutes, the conversation flowed, and Lady Drimmen glanced between the three younger people looking almost baffled.

"I heard a rumor you would sing tonight," Charles said to Sarah.

"If anyone wishes me to, I am happy to oblige," Sarah said at once. "But tonight is devoted chiefly to His Grace's discoveries."

"Speaking of which," Jenny said, "shall we go and look at them?"

Sarah glanced at her mother, who condescended to agree, and they made their way toward the display.

Lady Drimmen held Sarah back a moment, glancing toward Charles. "My dear, is that the heir to—"

"Yes," Sarah interrupted. "But we do not mention such matters here. As far as identity goes, we acknowledge only what an individual tells us. I am Miss Sarah, only, and Miss Hammond is Miss Hammy."

"Ramshackle," Lady Drimmen pronounced. "Though I suppose I am glad the world does not know my daughter is here."

Since the duke was in conversation, Sarah turned to examine the exhibits, several of which she had not seen before. But she was very aware when he turned from his conversation to greet her mother.

"My lady, what a pleasant surprise to find you and your husband here."

"Likewise, Your Grace. I see Drimmen is already soaking up your—er—pots."

"You might find these bracelets and buckles more interesting." He turned toward Sarah and her companions, and Sarah smiled. But he only nodded to them in general and moved on to speak to another group.

Hurt pierced her like the dagger she held in her hands. Hastily, she laid it down again, wondering miserably why he should be so cold when he had told her he would speak to her parents as soon as they arrived?

The answer, perhaps, was watching her from the other side of the room. Lady Loxley, beautiful, confident, and smiling as she made her graceful way toward them. Sarah braced herself for another war of words, but her ladyship walked straight past with the merest inclination of her head and took the duke's arm.

"My dear, come and meet someone I have been telling all about you," she purred.

And the duke, civilly excusing himself, walked away with her on his arm.

The dagger twisted.

"Miss Sarah, how charming you look, as always." Lord Trenton stood before her, smiling.

"And how flattering you are, sir, as always," Sarah managed to reply. "Mother, are you acquainted with Lord Trenton?"

Her mother extended one hand, which Trenton bowed over. "Indeed. But you just told me you do not use titles here."

"Alas, I am not part of the Whitmore community, my lady, merely its friend," Trenton explained.

"And generous donor," Sarah added.

"In truth, I do little," Trenton said deprecatingly. "May I fetch you a glass of wine, ladies?"

Lady Drimmen did look mildly impressed that an earl danced attendance on her daughter, but as the evening progressed, very little changed. Her parents must have noticed the marked improvement in her manners and social graces. They saw the way friends sought her out and talked to her with clear pleasure. Nearly everyone complimented her—and Lady Drimmen—on the wonder of her voice and looked forward to hearing her. But none of it seemed to alter their disapproval.

Worse than anything was that Leonard did not come near her. And she, hemmed in by her parents had little chance to go to him and ask what was wrong, what had changed…

What if Lady Loxley is right? Her blood ran cold with the thought. Could he really have said and done all these things merely to seduce her? And now that he had sampled the wares, as it were, and found them wanting in comparison, no doubt, to Maria Loxley's charm and experience… Was that it? Had he cynically talked himself into her bed and deserted her?

Her, Lady Sarah Merrington, the daughter of the Earl of Drimmen?

Surely, it was inconceivable?

Yes, she realized with a flood of relief. It *was* inconceivable. And not so much because of who *she* was, but because of who *he* was. Honest, honorable, and true.

And she would capture and keep his attention with her song, just as she had when he had first come here.

The pianoforte was in the next room, where people drifted after exclaiming over Leonard's Viking finds. Here there were poetry readings, including one from Mr. Granville that Sarah applauded enthusiastically. Miss Hammy was pink with pride in him.

At last the calls for Sarah to sing became too much, and Lady Whitmore bustled up and asked her if she would oblige.

"Of course," Sarah said, rising from her chair.

But her mother caught her wrist. "Don't, Sarah," she pleaded. "I could not bear…"

"I have to, Mother," Sarah said, hurt all over again. "I promised Lady Whitmore. You must cover your ears or leave the room."

Without Signor Arcadi, she had to accompany herself, but she had grown used to this during her frequent solitary practice at the cottage. Her fingers knew their way about the keys from memory, and she could concentrate on her voice.

She sang a sad, Scottish love song, and put her heart and soul into it. The threat of losing Leo so soon after she had found him must have lent authenticity for when she came to the end, she saw the sea of her audience's faces staring back at her in awe. One lady had tears on her cheeks. Lady Drimmen's mouth had dropped open. Her father was blinking rapidly.

And there at the back, was Leonard, unmoving, his gaze fixed on her, over the head of Lady Loxley who sat on the chair in front of him. At last, their eyes met, and a funny little smile curved his lips. Oh yes, there was tenderness there, and some rueful apology, something he was willing her to understand...

As the applause broke out, she stood, smiling and curtseying. But their clamor drove her back to the pianoforte and another song. She sang to the music she had found here at the castle the day Leonard had dropped her in the lake. This time, she noticed with pleasure the smile on her mother's face and recognized it as relief. Lady Drimmen had been genuinely afraid Sarah would make a fool of herself.

Only as she stood once more and walked away from the piano did she realize that Leonard had left the room. And Lady Loxley's chair was empty.

For the first time that evening, as she made her way through the admiring throngs, she deliberately avoided her parents. She forced herself to exchange civil words with everyone she spoke to, but the need to see Leonard would no longer be denied.

She swept through the display room, where lurked only a couple of serious, academic looking gentlemen, and out into the passage. Still there was no sign of him.

But as she turned her reluctant feet back

toward the salons, the cloakroom door opened, and Lady Loxley emerged in her elegant silk-lined cloak.

"Oh, are you leaving so early?" Sarah asked, instead of what she really wanted to know: *Where is Leonard?*

"Oh, we may be back," Lady Loxley said. "It depends how late Lady Whitmore closes her doors."

We? She would not ask. She wouldn't.

But Maria Loxley told her anyway, coming close enough to pat her hand with the sort of false, patronising sympathy that made Sarah itch to slap her.

"Leonard and I. An assignation for grown-ups. You have learned a difficult lesson, my dear, but at least your Mama is here to comfort you."

Sarah stared after her, unseeing. No. No, she would not believe it. She could not. Leonard *would* not.

And yet she had to admit she was naïve. That she could be wrong about Leo, about everything. He could have been wrong about her understanding. After all, she had, in the end, invited him to her bed. Did he despise her for that? Did it put her in the same category as Maria Loxley and the countless other women of his past?

Blood sang in her ears. She felt numb, helpless, abandoned. And yet so hemmed in she could not breathe.

"Miss Sarah?" Lord Trenton touched her elbow. "Is something wrong?"

"Everything," she whispered. "Everything is wrong. My lord…would you grant me a favor?"

"Anything," he replied instantly.

"Would you please lend me your carriage?"

MR. JAMES DID not care for people like Lady Loxley. Worldly, ambitious, totally selfish, and prepared to trample everyone in pursuit of their trivial goals.

He had, however, grown to care a great deal for his employer, and although he had made it a rule never to interfere in His Grace's personal life, he deemed it time to suspend that rule.

As a result, while Sarah melted everyone's heart with song and Leonard's expression told him all he needed to know, he bent and murmured in Lady Loxley's ear. He felt rather than saw her smile, but it was enough to know he had hooked her.

He slipped out of the castle with Sarah's angelic voice still ringing in his ears. Collecting one of the lanterns from the front door, he walked quickly to the edge of the lake, and sat down to await events.

She did not keep him long. She came eagerly,

though less gracefully than usual, trying to hold her skirts away from mud and foliage and still keep the lantern steady.

She must have seen his light, for she paused. "Leonard?"

"Here," James called, rising to his feet.

He saw the precise moment she recognized him by the ferocious frown tugging at her elegant brows.

"Where is His Grace?" she demanded without greeting.

"In the castle, I imagine."

"But you told me he would be here. Now."

"No, I said *you* should be. If you misunderstood the nature of the assignation, I can only apologize."

Her mouth fell open. "Do you seriously imagine I would consider you as a—"

"As an eligible lover?" he interrupted calmly. "No, of course I do not. I know my limitations, and yours. And the truth is, His Grace is *not* yours. He belongs heart and soul to another. You must know you cannot win him back now."

"You exceed your place, sirrah," she said contemptuously.

"Actually, I don't. I have finally realized that His Grace is correct when he calls me his friend. It is as his friend, not his secretary, that I speak now. You must not try to come between him and Sarah. It is cruel, hurtful, and will do none of you any good. Especially not you."

"Then why are you here?" she asked triumphantly. "If you do not fear me, why trouble to bring me here and persuade me?"

"Because you are resorting to blackmail. I want to give you the chance to take back your threats. After all, if you hurt her, you hurt him. Whether you keep her from him or tell the world about her indiscretion, he will never forgive you."

"I don't want his forgiveness," she snapped. "I want his rank and his lands and the life he will give me. The rest, even the Merrington girl, will matter nothing to him in time. I am, you know, very persuasive."

"So, you will not budge?"

"I will not."

James sighed. "Then I must tell you that your own indiscretions are noted. I know, for example, that you visited Trenton in his bedchamber more than once."

She stared. "I did not touch Trenton! He is a boy."

"The world does not know that. But even so, it is but one of many indiscretions. And I have seen the way you pursue the duke. In short, my lady, I have it in my power to make you a laughing stock."

She laughed. "You? You are a nobody!"

"That is true. I am nobody. But I know *every*body. All of His Grace's family and friends. All his servants. It would not take many words to spread a story, a jest."

She stared at him. "You would not dare."

"I am his friend," James said simply. "I want him to be happy, and I know where his happiness lies."

Her lips curled. "So, it comes down to which of us can out-extort the other?"

"If you like. I need your word, my lady, that you will stop this."

"And if I refuse?"

"Then I shall push you in the lake and drop a word in the ear of His Grace's valet. He knows all the gentlemen's gentlemen. That should ensure you return to London with the wrong kind of attention."

She considered him. "I shall not care when I am Duchess of Vexen. And your Sarah a never-to-be-married whore."

"You will never be Duchess of Vexen. The question is really whether or not your reputation survives to win a different husband."

"I don't believe you," she said flatly. "And I refuse."

With that, she turned her back. And James, with the slightest nudge, toppled her into the lake.

She shrieked with as much cold as rage, and James leaned down, grasping her flailing hand, and hauled her out.

"You see?" he said. "I always keep my word. I'll send His Grace's carriage to the foot of the drive to convey you to the inn. My lips remain sealed until the morning. Good night." He tipped his hat to her dripping, gasping person and walked smartly back to the drive.

Rather pleased with his night's work, he re-entered the castle, tossed his hat on to the stand by the door, and leapt upstairs toward the salons.

Halfway up the staircase, he met the duke coming down. His face was white and devastated.

"I've lost Sarah," he blurted. "She's gone."

"Gone?" James repeated blankly.

The duke dragged his hand through his hair, tugging at it. "I tried to keep Maria off her back by staying away from her, but the upshot is she has run away with Trenton!"

CHAPTER SEVENTEEN

A S SARAH STOOD with Lord Trenton at the
end of the driveway, ready to climb in his
carriage and make her escape from everything
and everyone she loved, the sound of a woman
wailing, caterwauling really, made both her and
Trenton uncomfortable.

"You haven't much time, Lady Sarah," Trenton said, looking about, obviously concerned that
someone would see them leaving together.

Sarah knew time was short, but... "We cannot flee if there is a woman in peril, my lord. As
much as I wish to, can we please find out what is
wrong? Where the screaming is coming from?"

Trenton frowned, but nodded, then grabbed
one of the lanterns hanging on the carriage. He
gestured for his servants to wait and offered his
arm to Sarah. "If we follow the noise, I am sure
we will find our victim down by the lake."

Grateful for his company and friendship,

Sarah gripped his arm and walked with him, sincerely worried for whoever was yelling out in pain.

They reached the lakeside and found her—Lady Maria standing alone, wet and shivering, lily pads hanging from the length of her hair that had tumbled from its pins, furious and, quite frankly, inconsolable.

"How dare you bring her here, Trenton!" she screamed. "Have you chosen her over me, too? Decided to complete my humiliation?"

Lord Trenton stared at her with absolute horror. "Madame, we would not be here if it weren't for Lady Sarah's sincere concern. She insisted we find the woman in peril—to help—not humiliate."

Lady Maria's hands balled into fists as she glared at Sarah. "You will never amount to anything, you graceless whore. A duchess? Did you really think Leonard would…"

"Stop!" Trenton said firmly, stepping forward. "Say no more, Maria."

"Or what?" Her hostile gaze swept to him. "Have you tumbled into her bed, too? Sampled what the duke took once and walked away from? You never struck me as the sort of man who would settle for sloppy seconds."

The words wounded Sarah so deeply, she gasped in shock. But she would not shrink away from this woman, not now. Not when so much hung in the balance. Her future happiness, Leonard's joy, their lives together.

She walked directly up to Maria. "Everything you say is steeped in lies, manipulation to make yourself feel better. You are not superior, Lady Maria, you are afraid of being alone."

At first, Maria scoffed at her, looking her up and down. "You know nothing."

"I know enough," Sarah countered. "I know that I love His Grace, and all you want from him is a title and his wealth. You care nothing about him. Admit it!"

Lady Maria laughed. "What is one duke over another? I am fortunate Leonard is pleasing to look at."

"He is not for you," Lord Trenton gritted out. "Now, let us get you back to the inn, so you do not catch your death out here." He started to shrug out of his coat.

"No!" Maria screamed even louder. "I want everyone to know what this girl has done. How she stole my betrothed from me by seducing him!"

Someone emerged from the shadows, and as Sarah focused on the large form, she suddenly realized...Leonard. How long had he been standing there? Had he heard everything?

When Maria saw him, she quieted down, possibly ashamed, or more likely caught.

"Lady Maria," he said sternly. "What are you

about?"

She hugged her middle, shivering and suddenly humbled. "I have done nothing but defend my honor, Leonard."

"You are not so familiar with me, madame," he chastised her.

"Your Grace," she quickly corrected herself.

Sarah closed her eyes and took a deep breath. This should never have happened, never. Now her dreams were dashed, for the duke would not even look at her, didn't even acknowledge her presence. And her parents, they would take her away.

Her fears materialized, for Lady Whitmore, Mr. James, and her parents joined them.

"What is this about?" Sarah's father demanded, eyeing his daughter, Lady Maria, and Lord Trenton. "Why are you dressed for travel, Sarah? Were you and Lord Trenton going to elope? We saw the carriage at the end of the drive, and it belongs to his lordship."

"Sarah!" her mother said, giving her a scathing look of disapproval, then swooning. "How could you do this to us? Have we not indulged you, given you everything you've wished for?"

"Lady Drimmen," Lady Whitmore intervened. "I am afraid you do not give your lovely daughter enough credit."

"Yes," Leonard suddenly turned around and walked in front of Sarah, shielding her with his body. "Your daughter is innocent, Lord and Lady Drimmen. She is my betrothed, and I am a fool."

Sarah's father stared at her, speechless at first. "Your betrothed, you say, Your Grace?"

"No!" Lady Maria yelled, rushing to the forefront.

"Lady Maria," Leonard growled in warning. "You are in no position to challenge anyone. Have you not said enough already?"

"Yes." Lady Whitmore took her arm. "Let Lord Trenton and I escort you back to the inn. You are wet and cold, not thinking clearly at all."

Lady Maria looked about, first at Leonard, then at Sarah and her parents. She shrugged and laughed. "You are but a duke," she said to Leonard. "And not even a very good one."

Lord Trenton shook his head as he scooped Maria into his arms and carried her away with Lady Whitmore at his side. That left Sarah, the man she loved, Mr. James, and her parents alone together. An uncomfortable silence settled over them, and Sarah wondered what her father would do, if he'd give his permission for her to marry Leonard.

The duke turned to her, resting his strong, warm hands on her shoulders and gazing into her eyes, the intensity of his stare arousing every emotion she could possibly feel. "I am sorry, my love," he said softly. "I let someone come between us because I feared the implications on you. Lady Maria is an opportunist and a brutal one at that. Can you forgive me?"

"Forgive you?" Tears streamed down her cheeks. "There is nothing to forgive, Your Grace. You have been honorable and honest with me from the start. I toyed with your heart. I owe you an apology."

Leonard grinned and then pulled her into his arms, kissing the top of her head and then tipping her face up with his fingers. "Have I told you how much I love you, Sarah?"

She shook her head.

"No?" he asked.

"No."

"Well then, let us remedy that now." His mouth claimed hers, and his tongue teased her lips apart, kissing her with unbridled passion, undeniable love.

"Sarah!" her mother called insistently. "This is a disgrace."

"Lady Drimmen," Sarah heard her father say firmly. "For once in your life, will you be quiet?"

LEONARD COULD NOT keep himself from laughing at Lord Drimmen's words, and the kiss was cut short. But there was so much more to come with his beautiful bride-to-be, so much more. He pulled away from her and rested his forehead against hers. "Do you forgive me, sweeting?"

"Of course," she whispered.

He nodded his approval. "Mr. James?"

"Your Grace?" His secretary came forth, having held his tongue this whole time. Leonard would increase his salary as soon as everything was settled.

"Do you have the special license?"

"I do, Your Grace."

"Thank you," Leonard said. Then, he dropped to his knee and took something from his pocket, looking up at Sarah.

"Your Grace?" She covered her mouth with both hands.

"Do not look so surprised, Lady Sarah. We have done this before, I think. But now everything is in order, and is this not part of my duties as your future husband?"

"Yes."

He took one of her hands and kissed her knuckles and the inside of her wrist. "Will you do me the honor of becoming my best friend, my lover, my duchess, and my wife? I promise we will face the world together, Sarah. No one will come between us again."

"Yes, Your Grace. Yes."

He slid the sapphire and diamond ring onto her dainty finger, then rose to his feet, opening his arms to her. She crashed into him, and he closed his arms around her, protective and feeling like a besotted fool. There was nowhere else he'd rather be.

"Do you know, my sweet," he said, resting his chin on the top of her head. "I believe I will ask your father to let my estate manager dig up that apple tree from his property and transplant it to our home."

"What tree?" Lord Drimmen asked.

"The apple tree, Father," Sarah said. "The one you said disgraced our family."

Her father coughed exaggeratedly before he came to stand next to Sarah and the duke. "Your Grace," he said, "you can have the blasted tree and anything else you want. Just promise to take care of my girl."

"Oh, Father!" Sarah threw her arms around him, and Leonard fought to keep his eyes dry as even Lady Drimmen offered her congratulations to her daughter.

"Shall we go back to the house?" Leonard offered. "I believe Lady Whitmore has an excellent bottle of champagne waiting for us."

Together, Leonard and his bride and her parents strolled back to the castle.

Whitmore was everything his mother had promised, a truly magical place. And Leonard would do everything he could to make sure Sarah and his mother, and now the sister he so desperately wanted to find, were loved and protected forever.

CHAPTER EIGHTEEN

I T SEEMED LADY Whitmore truly was a miracle worker.

Sarah had imagined, in a dazed kind of way, that she and Leonard would be married quietly in the library or some other private room in the castle after the guests had departed.

But as Leonard opened the salon door, a sea of faces turned and smiled indulgently. A path seemed to have been left for them, leading through the throng to Mr. Grantley, the local vicar. Beside him, Lady Whitmore smiled and stood back.

The vicar bowed slightly, as though welcoming their approach. Sarah cast one, wild look at Leonard, who merely placed her hand on his arm once more and led her forward.

Although her body seemed to move mechanically, her heart filled as she realized all her friends were here, everyone who had become so important to her over the last two years—all the poets and musicians, painters, and sculptors whose true identities she had never needed to know. And there was Hammy, dear Hammy, weeping and smiling, supported by Mr. Granville.

Behind her, her parents followed, then stood beside Lady Whitmore as Sarah and Leonard faced the vicar.

The ceremony was short and simple and beautiful. Somewhere, Sarah could not quite believe she was actually marrying Leonard. Her responses and promises were made with an air of surprise, and she could not take her eyes off the man to whom she willingly gave herself. Leonard's words were firm and spoken directly as he gazed into her eyes.

And then Mr. Grantley declared them man and wife, and she was the Duchess of Vexen.

Laughter began to bubble its way through her daze. She clung to his hand, smiling as she received the best wishes of the company. A glass of champagne was thrust into her free hand, and then Lady Whitmore led everyone into the dining room.

Sarah was at the door before she registered the music playing them out of the room. On impulse, she stopped and gazed toward the pianoforte.

Signor Arcadi inclined his head, a faint, rueful smile on his lips. And yet the old arrogance was still there. Sarah laughed and raised her glass to him in a silent toast. There was no grudge to bear against the man who had given her so much.

The wedding breakfast—or wedding supper, she supposed—was fresh joy to Sarah. She felt as if she loved the whole world. Even her mother looked proud of her. And yet, having finally won that pride, she realized it didn't matter. She loved her anyway, in spite of criticism or approval. It was a merry feast, as sparkling as the champagne, which flowed so liberally. At her side, Leonard seemed increasingly large and warm and desirable.

This was her wedding night.

As though he heard her thought, Leonard rose suddenly to his feet and swept up his glass.

"Join me if you will in a final toast of the evening," he said. "To our kind hostess, who has made everything possible. And to family, near and far."

He tossed the wine down his throat as the others enthusiastically echoed his words, and set his glass on the table with curious determination.

He held out his hand to Sarah. His eyes glittered.

"Your Grace," he said softly.

Suddenly, she couldn't breathe. She was his duchess, his bride. Her hand trembled as she placed it in his, but she smiled around the table with happiness and pride as she walked out on his arm.

Excitement was growing, for tonight, he would make love to her again…

As he closed the bedchamber door behind him, she examined her surroundings. His subtle scent was all around her. His room was cluttered with things she associated with him—books and papers, odd little tools, broken pieces he had retrieved from his site, and not yet repaired.

She turned into his arms.

"No regrets?" he murmured, stroking her hair.

She shook her head. "None."

"Maria Loxley is firmly in my past. I'm afraid there were others, too."

"I know, but you don't have to explain."

"Don't worry, I don't mean to sully your ears with a list of my sordid indiscretions. I only mention them to explain that it is all in my past. You are everything, now and forever."

She smiled, smoothing her fingertips over his frown. "I know." She did, although she could not explain it. Her doubts, her jealousies, had all vanished. "The game has not ended quite as I planned it."

"Hasn't it?" He lowered his head and kissed her, thoroughly enough to deprive her of breath.

"I don't know anymore," she whispered. "I was so foolish, so obsessed… Perhaps I always knew we should be together, and that was why I was so hurt when you left. It doesn't matter now."

"What does matter?" he asked, his gentle, deft fingers busy with the lacings of her gown.

"You and I. This moment."

Her gown slid to the floor, along with her stays. In one swift, pleasantly shocking movement, he swept off her chemise, and she stood before him in only her stockings. Heat curled in her stomach and blazed from his hungry eyes.

She felt like a siren, irresistible and powerful and *his*. She wrapped her arms around his neck and pressed herself against him.

"Make me your duchess," she whispered.

He took her mouth, lifting her in his arms. "With the greatest pleasure…"

About Mary Lancaster

Mary Lancaster lives in Scotland with her husband, three mostly grown-up kids and a small, crazy dog.

Her first literary love was historical fiction, a genre which she relishes mixing up with romance and adventure in her own writing. Her most recent books are light, fun Regency romances written for Dragonblade Publishing: *The Imperial Season* series set at the Congress of Vienna; and the popular *Blackhaven Brides* series, which is set in a fashionable English spa town frequented by the great and the bad of Regency society.

Connect with Mary on-line – she loves to hear from readers:

Email Mary:
Mary@MaryLancaster.com

Website:
www.MaryLancaster.com

Newsletter sign-up:
http://eepurl.com/b4Xoif

Facebook:
facebook.com/mary.lancaster.1656

Facebook Author Page:
facebook.com/MaryLancasterNovelist

Twitter:
@MaryLancNovels

Amazon Author Page:
amazon.com/Mary-Lancaster/e/B00DJ5IACI

Bookbub:
bookbub.com/profile/mary-lancaster

About Violetta Rand

Raised in Corpus Christi, Texas, Violetta Rand spent her childhood reading, writing, and playing soccer. After meeting her husband in New England, they moved to Alaska where she studied environmental science. Violetta spent a decade working as a scientist before quitting her day job to pursue her dream as a full time writer.

Violetta still lives in Anchorage, Alaska, and spends her days writing evocative contemporary and historical romance. When she's not reading, writing, or editing, she enjoys time with her husband, pets, and friends.

Website:
www.violettarandromance.com